MORE PRAISE FOR *Desire*

"*Desire* is a lyrical, funny and poignant road trip. If Kerouac were a sexy waif of a girl, this is the book he would write."
—JAMIE CALLAN

"No description of this novel will do its quiet vision justice. Lindsay Ahl's forthright lyricism creates a landscape as mysterious as it is persuasive, as sturdy as it is ethereal."
—ABBY FRUCHT

"Lindsay Ahl catches the voice of a generation, avid for life and soured on the mistakes and ineptitude of parents who failed to save an endangered world." —MARK JAY MIRSKY

"*Desire* contains a lusty cinematic intensity, conveying an uneasy tale of sexual liberties and repression as well as the lies we tell our lovers." —ERNESTO QUIÑONEZ

"Poetical, surreal and unnervingly beautiful, *Desire* is a novel that breathes life into the reader."
—FREDERIC TUTEN

DESIRE

A NOVEL

BY LINDSAY AHL

COFFEE HOUSE PRESS

2004

Coffee House Press books are available to the trade through our primary distributor, Consortium Book Sales & Distribution, 1045 Westgate Drive, Saint Paul, MN 55114. For personal orders, catalogs, or other information, write to: Coffee House Press, 27 North Fourth Street, Suite 400, Minneapolis, MN 55401.

Coffee House Press is a nonprofit literary publishing house. Support from private foundations, corporate giving programs, government programs, and generous individuals help make the publication of our books possible. We gratefully acknowledge their support in detail in the back of this book.

To you and our many readers across the country, we send our thanks for your continuing support.

Good books are brewing at coffeehousepress.org

LIBRARY OF CONGRESS CIP DATA

Ahl, Lindsay.
Desire / a novel / by Lindsay Ahl.
p. cm.
ISBN 1-56689-154-x (alk. paper)
1. Americans—Kenya—Fiction. 2. Mothers and daughters—Fiction.
3. Child witnesses—Fiction. 4. Women—Kenya—Fiction.
5. Ivory industry—Fiction. 6. Kenya—Fiction. I. Title.
PS3601.H55D47 2004
813'.6—DC22
2004002893

FIRST EDITION | FIRST PRINTING
1 3 5 7 9 10 8 6 4 2

PRINTED IN CANADA

DESIRE

1

I have such a craving for one of those small cold bottles of Concord grape juice that I leave Michael's house at around six in the morning and head toward the 7–Eleven, which is always open twenty-four hours a day. The air is fresh and warm but still damp, before the sun has burned it dry, and there's no one around. I take the alleyway behind Michael's house, a dirt road that begins with a cottonwood tree and travels behind houses with chain-link fences and clotheslines and barking dogs. I notice in the yard across from a white apartment complex that someone has thrown out an African sculpture. I stand close and peer through the metal fence, just staring at the object from different angles, until finally I realize it's just an old rawhide dog bone. This delay displaces me. I switch my course at the new Kinko's and step over a low chain at the edge of the parking lot.

Around here, by the university, every street has a back alley. If I were to map the area, Albuquerque would have a whole mini-city within itself, a shadow grid of roads—some dirt, some paved—that run behind houses, laundromats, ice cream stores, parking lots. Maybe these alleys are for the telephone poles, because that's where most of them are, the long wires a resting spot for blackbirds. As I walk, I take an alley, then a street, then another alley, zigzagging through the grid in the direction of wherever I'm going.

The alley that runs parallel to Central Avenue has been blocked off by a fence, some construction project. It's impractical to double-back to 7–Eleven so I just cut through the Burger King lot.

There are police sirens in the distance as I walk across, crunching the gravel in the flowerbeds by the order intercom. Underneath the bushes to my right, in the landscaping of the drive-thru, I see a glint in the rocks. It is a white mini Bic, a lighter, brand-new. I pause to pick it up, flick the knob to start the little flame, and cross over to the drive-thru area.

There, against the back wall of Burger King is a man rolling in fire, not saying anything, not moaning or screaming, just rolling and jerking the newspapers around himself. He is alive and on fire, and I just stand there. He is the neighborhood drunk, usually drooling and smelling of vomit and rotting flesh, and if you happen to be so unlucky as to not be able to cross the street but have to pass by him on the sidewalk where he sprawls, he hisses at you, like a snake. He is not someone I have any desire to get close to, even to put out the fire that is consuming him. So I stand there and watch. And besides, I can see even now a police car, wailing its siren and pulling up fast. The man stops moving. He remains completely still for several seconds, during which time my horror kicks in. I am standing here doing nothing. And then I notice, through the crazy lights of the fire engine that pulls up, the manager of Burger King, leaning onto the side of the building about twenty feet away from me.

By the time I run over, the police officer is already swatting the burning man with a coat. Between swats, he speaks into his crackly radio: static, words, more static. Empty bottles of Everclear and tequila are lined up against the wall, blackened and cracked from the heat. The man's canvas coat has burned badly, but his pants are some kind of polyester blend that have melted as much as burned, clinging to him darkly, except where parts of his skin peek through, raw and pink. It seems pretty obvious that he buried himself under the newspapers, poured liquor over it all, and set fire to himself, and that's what the police are saying to each other, *crazy drunkard*, to anyone around who will listen. I get a chance to step up close, and look into the man's wide-open eyes.

His body stinks intensely and I want to back off. It smells like a body that is already decomposing. I feel dizzy. He probably hasn't bathed in months. I want to look away, walk away, but I stand there and stare. I look at his face, the least damaged of all of him, blackened and melted only over one ear.

The Burger King manager is laughing a bit. "Disgusting," he says. "He passed out last week, in the bathroom, and I had to call the cops. Remember?" He points to one of the policemen. "I called you."

The burned man's eyes are wide open, an unremarkable sky blue, rolled back a little, though not as much as you'd think. But in his eyes, after a moment, I see a man in a trap. He was in a trap the moment he died. It's terrifying: a little blue fire of life, still fighting; a conscious man fighting for his life.

In the back of my mind, completely unrelated to anything going on around me, I hear a vague screaming. It lasts for only a second. I break out in a cold sweat and I almost throw up. But I'm not the type of person who is so weak as to faint at the sight of a dead person. I collect myself. I look at the man.

I yell to the policeman. I think I yell, "Hey."

"What?"

I point, and he doesn't see it or maybe he does, because he bends down and closes the fire-blue eyes of the burned man. Thin, tiny weaves of clear polyester in the cop's blue suit shine out at me in the sun, and for one second I smell his cologne, a musky Aramis.

"You smoke?" he asks, nodding to the Bic in my left hand, cupped in my palm. I had pointed to the burned man's eyes with it.

"What? Oh, I found it over there in the gravel. By the inter-com." I point.

The policeman takes the lighter from me and holds its small height between his thumb and forefinger.

"Do you smoke?"

"No, sir," I answer.

"So why did you pick it up?"

"Um. I don't know. It was reflecting the light, you know, shining out at me." I shrug, a bad habit I've recently picked up from Michael, who shrugs a lot, usually for no good reason. I've told him that this is some weird excessive gesture of his, but he doesn't care.

The policeman nods and looks at me. "Mind if I see your I.D.?"

I reach into my bag and find my license.

"You know," I say, nervous, snapping the cold plastic rectangle into his hand, "I guess it looks weird, but I was just walking along, and then I saw him—"

"It's all right," he says, looking at my license for one second and then handing it back to me, "but I might have to call you as a witness."

I nod.

"And I have to keep this," he says, holding up the Bic.

I continue walking, in a kind of daze, across Central Avenue and over to the anthropology office. I classify and describe petroglyphs in a third-floor air-conditioned office for a woman who drinks Snapple iced tea for lunch and is never without a scarf and several jingling bracelets. She tells me I have an eye for petroglyphs. I kind of doubt I have an eye for petroglyphs, but for a while they interested me. There are several debates taking place about exactly how to interpret petroglyphs, and I enjoy the dissension. Usually I project slides of the latest petroglyphs onto high-resolution aerial photographs and search for various data. For example, I find all the life-sized spear throwers within two meters of masks. Or I take notes on direction: if a petroglyph is on the north side of a canyon, what is on the south side? Often the masks face south, and the spear throwers face north. I personally don't think this is a coincidence.

I used to work out in the field, plotting maps using global positioning units to show where various petroglyphs are located, and that's where I met Michael, and it is Michael who convinced me to stay with this job. We actually met on location. Our office was stationed for two weeks in Specter Canyon, part of Canyonlands National Park. It's a two-hour drive on a dirt road west of Moab, Utah, and about a five-hour hike down a canyon. The day I decided I wasn't interested in petroglyphs was the day we were documenting a whole wall of larger-than-life, cloaked, floating human-faced figures. To me, it was obvious these were pictures of the dead—receding, coming forward, burnt red in the sandstone. Myself, I could hear them rasping, like the ever-present wind, and I rounded the corner, to be away from it all, and on the next mesa over I could see women calling out, wind lashing their hair, skirts blowing wildly; they were waiting to jump; embracing their death.

Naturally, I said nothing; my visions are not scientific. But a few minutes later Michael came around the bend in the canyon, looking like the kind of guy who knows, as well as I do, that the world has already ended. We have never discussed this. But at that moment, he motioned with his hand, his cream-colored shirt wavy in the heat, and told me that directly across this canyon, five miles south, there were several of the largest spirals he had ever seen. What did I make of that?

I shivered. I hate spirals. I tried to focus on the shape of his chest under his shirt.

As I walk into the office, my boss hands me, with a hand that won't stop trembling, thin, badly reproduced photos of Specter Canyon. I think she laces her Snapple with vodka. I sift through them as she mumbles, "All the information lost in just a few generations," over and over again, and then straightens her back and leaves like she just thought of something important to do.

I feel overwhelmed, and don't want to sit down. Specter Canyon was not something I wanted to work on today. Perhaps the burned man poisoned me. By breathing in his burning body I have taken in his poisoned spirit.

I call Michael, who is out in the field.

"You know that homeless man, the drunk guy, the one who spits? Well, I saw him burn to death this morning," I say.

"What?"

"I just stood around and watched. But he had this look in his eyes. After he died. Like—"

"How did it happen?" Michael's voice is thin, he's focusing on something else; besides that, his cell phone is erratic.

I give him the details but then I try to tell him something else. I tell him the man was in a trap, that he didn't know he would die that day.

"Oh please," Michael sighs, "just focus on the facts."

I refrain from telling him that the facts I know never seem to have in and of themselves any particular consequence; it is only in how they are interlinked, how they change and alter the other facts around them, that gives you a full picture. I am interested in the full picture. I've rarely found a genuine fact, complete with the weight of objectivity, or a history that is unalterable. Facts are so complex and subtle, so deceptive and slippery, that I doubt their ability to elucidate the truth.

I've always told everyone: my mother died in Africa in 1975. Her name was Elena Monroe. She had straight brown hair to her waist, wore polka-dotted miniskirts, and painted every kitchen she ever lived in black and white. This is what I know about Africa in 1975: the price of ivory was thirty-five dollars a pound, although seven years before, in 1968, it was only three dollars a pound, and by 1980 in Japan the price would rise to two hundred dollars a pound. In 1975, one large tusk was worth seven thousand dollars; by 1980, the same tusk would be worth forty thousand dollars. Ivory became more precious than gold, and at least seventy thousand elephants a year were killed, more than eighty percent shot by poachers.

I happen to own several tiny carved ivory elephants, and an ivory bracelet. My stepfather, Dr. Sam Fraizer, bought them for me in Bamako, Mali, when we lived there, when I was nine. Sam probably didn't know about the elephants being poached; he was doing follow-up research on the smallpox vaccinations he had advocated and performed a few years before.

It was Sam who gave my mother her first camera, so that she could help with photographing his "clients," as he called them, though really they were just smallpox or polio victims whom he sought out for his research.

While Sam was at work in another country, Elena got fed up and left. We traveled by boat to Timbuktu, and there she met Forester Ecco, who took us to his house in Kenya.

When I received a letter from Forester Ecco three weeks ago, it was addressed to Elena Monroe. It has always been a great burden to me that my name is the same as hers. I find a mother who could name her daughter after herself somehow inexcusably narcissistic. Forester's letter arrived in my mailbox along with a *Have You Seen Me?* postcard with photos of missing children and a blue envelope full of discount coupons.

The letter is written on thin paper that is beginning to tatter because I carry it around with me everywhere. The letter from Forester is a fact like an action, it doesn't stay still, it causes the ground to sink and rise beneath my feet. It is a fact like Michael's water walk, his macaw's yellow stare, the blackbirds gathering in the graveyard behind my apartment—they all are signs I can't read. They all feed my suspicion that every little motion of the world so obviously signifies something else.

When I get out of work, I walk across Central Avenue and up Zuni to wait for Michael on the steps in the sun, where, usually around 5:00 P.M. he either drives up, or slides down the railing of the stairs and lands like a cat at my feet, occasionally with someone from his office, in which case we go out for dinner or to a movie, or if he's alone, we walk down the arroyo that runs all the way past the graveyard behind my apartment complex. Today he arrives on time, at my feet, wearing the usual—a sweaty but expensive white button-down shirt, untucked, jeans, boots, a leather jacket. He looks tired, his eyes have a dark rim beneath them. He kisses me for a minute, deep, like slipping into a lake.

"Hey," he says.

"Hey."

"Like your dress."

"You've seen it before."

He bumps up against me as we walk. "I'm starving. Let's go eat."

We walk down the street with all the restaurants and he doesn't choose one and I don't say anything; I just follow him through the alleyways where the light is long and pale gold. After a while we trudge down into the arroyo beside the graveyard.

"Where are we going?" I ask.

"I don't know. Someplace new," he says. "I saw a rattler today. That was fun. He must have been ten feet long."

We take a few tunnels, then hike the embankment up and out. Chamisa rubs off yellow on his jeans and my legs. We come out on a street I never walk on with tract housing and no restaurant in sight. But at the corner, we see Miguel's, a bar next to an abandoned gas station. Inside, the air is damp and dark, with only small colored squares of glass for windows.

There are a few people at the bar, no one at the tables.

"You been here before?" I ask him.

"No," he says, and since there is no food, he just orders two shots of tequila, and the waiter doesn't ask to see my I.D., which means this feeling of time not really passing isn't true.

When the glasses arrive, short and cased in leather pouches, the swirling amber liquid shining, his eyes fix on mine the same way Elena's used to, with a kind of velocity as they look away (or is it just vacuity?), filled with the same search and question.

"So what else did you do today," he asks, "besides watch the man burn?"

I pause too long. He orders us each another shot.

"What I did—all I did—was think about you," he says, reaching his arm across the table.

I think maybe he doesn't actually say this, because after the second shot I've entered a golden haze, like the rain in Africa, so that when Michael slams his shot glass down onto the wet rim of his napkin with a precise sweep of his arm, his eyes following the same motion, I see Elena, swirling a glass of wine in her hand, her eyes red, leaning into the doorway of a rotted-out hotel in Timbuktu, watching me as I run into the dunes, into a blurred and endless point on the horizon, her voice calling to me as I run, her words a dome of rising heat, the sand shifting under my feet.

Michael's hand slides along my arm. "You're not listening?" he asks, shaking the hair from his eyes.

"I'm distracted." I push my glass away and impulsively take his hand, pulling him toward the sign that says *Damas*.

I push him down the hallway past a cigarette machine and pay phone and into the bathroom. I lock the latch. A bucket and mop stand in one corner, smelling faintly of disinfectant, but mostly I stay close to his leather jacket and tequila breath.

His leather and zippers are like an alligator twisting in my arms, scuffling soft on the tiles. The sink presses cold against my back. His kisses are hard, his unshaved face scratches my cheeks and neck, and with his alligator breath he rips off my underwear and I tear off the first layer of his skin, throwing the carcass of his jacket to the floor.

We wrestle downward, his breathing heavy and distracting. I am above him, straddling him on the floor, my boots slipping, my dress around my hips as his hands glide up my body, his arms flexing. I notice he is not looking at me, but at the ceiling, his eyes like the horizon. And there, in the distance, on the far edge of the lake, are the elephants, roving blue-gray near the water. Elena loads film into one camera, and Forester takes that camera and hands her another. Forester Ecco is her new man. He has taken us far from Timbuktu, to his ranch, eighty miles outside of Nairobi. I look from my mother to the elephants, eight of them, an isolated family. Their ears are wide and flapping, until the wind shifts and they pause, curling their trunks upward, smelling.

I want to let go with Michael. He is looking at me now, watching my body. The sweat breaks out on my neck, my thighs. I can feel the strange flutter of my eyelids when my mind is almost disengaged. I am about to disappear into Michael.

The largest elephant is charging, running straight at us, her ears flying out, her size increasing rapidly. But Forester knows she won't ram into the Land Rover because Forester knows this elephant. She always stops short. They call her Helen, and, at thirty-three years old, she is the matriarch of the group.

Michael is looking at me now, his warm hands holding my ribs. I can see his face, but I am watching the elephant as she charges, her ears open wide; she is looking at me as though I am the only one in the truck, she is *condemning* me, running toward me, right when the deafening crack takes her to her knees and immobilizes the rest with confusion and fear. And one second later, all of the elephants are fumbling, unmoving, the baby at the back falling last.

I climb out of the Land Rover and run; I will save them, run in front of the bullets. I will be the earth, holding them up.

"Shit," I hear my mother yell.

"I'll get her." Forester runs up behind me.

I run toward the already dead elephants, which loom up larger and larger so that they become the horizon, so that there is nothing but elephant. The ground beneath the matriarch fills with blood, smelling. And the wind is already blowing her dust across my skin, across the dry earth.

"I told you already," Forester says, swinging me over his shoulder and carrying me back to the truck, "the elephants will starve."

I say nothing because it doesn't matter.

"She doesn't understand, Elena," he says.

"She understands," my mother answers. "She just doesn't like blood."

I stand up, move away from Michael.

"I can't," I say.

"What? What are you doing?"

"Finish," I say. "I can't finish."

His body lies there, his black hair on the grimy floor. I lean into the cold sink, my legs trembling.

"The floor is dirty," I tell him.

I fix my hair, swipe on some lipstick, and walk past, leaving him lying on the bathroom floor, listening to the toilet that has been running the entire time.

"You're always holding back," he yells through the door.

This seems rather strange to me: after I fell in love I couldn't orgasm.

For as long as Michael and I were essentially strangers, I was ready for any kind of a ride. But after I fell in love with him, my body rebelled. For a while I thought it was because I loved Michael too much. In many ways love and sex don't mix. And for a while I thought maybe it was better this way, just enjoyment without the release, perpetual pure pleasure with no outcome.

I started thinking—never mind multiple orgasms, go for sustained desire. Don't commit, because to commit is to let go of all you are holding on to. To commit is to say yes, and if you say yes, anything can happen. If you say yes, you can accidentally travel too far in the wrong direction. And if you travel too far in the wrong direction, your identity as you know it falters; you become unbalanced.

Then the whole thing seemed like just another sign I couldn't read.

I leave Miguel's bar and cross over the flat pale road with the tract housing and walk back down into the arroyo, then to the top end of the cemetery. The birds call in long cool gusts as they sit in the cottonwood trees.

"Wait up." I hear Michael running after me.

"I'm sorry," I say. "I'm distracted lately."

He shrugs.

I moved into the cheap apartment complex on the other side of the graveyard because I was in a rush to find someplace. I had only one day, and I could hear the blackbirds from the apartment. Thousands of blackbirds live in the graveyard all day, and every evening they fly down to the Rio Grande. I know because I've followed them in my car. Their sound is a distinctive guttural yell, and in each call they seem to let out the emotion of the world, which I admire these days, when I equate letting out the emotion of the world with orgasm.

"I'll be deaf," I think he says, but it's hard to hear over the screaming birds.

He yells, waving his arms, and hundreds of blackbirds rise up, making static in the sky. As soon as we pass by, they settle back in their trees, their cries changing from the desperate cry of warning to a short repetitive cooing, low in their throat, *take me take me take me.*

It is only a fifteen-minute walk from the bar to the parking lot of my building, but halfway there the sky billows up, dark gray, and we are under a cold smattering rain. We continue walking normally for a few minutes, Michael holding my hand. And then it is too much, we're drenched and cold, so we run across the graveyard and rush into my studio apartment. I live on the second floor and my one window overlooks the parking lot. The walls are thin and three doors down a guy is yelling at his girlfriend again. About once a month the cops have to bust them up.

"Try not to step on them," I say, pointing vaguely to the dozens of xeroxes that cover my floor. Petroglyph research. "And don't get them wet," I say. "They'll wrinkle."

"You're stepping on them," he says.

"But I know *where* to step."

"Can't you just pick them up? Put them somewhere?"

"Well, no."

"All right," he says, slowly. His hair is wet and dripping, following the curves of his skull. We are standing near the closet, taking off wet clothes and replacing them with dry, and he touches me, his hand on my shoulder, sliding down my naked back.

"I don't know why . . ." he begins, and I tense up. My whole body just freezes. I feel like I just became another person, or that I'm suddenly not here. I'm in a dark field.

"Can you . . . go now?" I ask.

He looks at me.

"Really?"

I nod yes. I want him to go forever or promise to stay forever, but I can't say that, and then I can't say anything, I'm too sad, and he knows this, but is already leaving anyway, pulling on a dry but dirty shirt that he left here long ago, leaving his wet shirt on the closet floor.

Even amazing facts, like for example, facts about elephants, eyewitness observations about how elephants in zoos will play with the faucets, how they love to paint, how they get bored, or, in the wild, how they mourn their dead by placing leaves and branches over dead bodies, and seem in fact to have an anticipation and dread of death, or how a male bull walks easily 150 miles a day and will get painful and crippling arthritis if not allowed to walk a great deal, or the more technical facts, like the elephant penis averages four feet long and weighs sixty pounds—these add up to nothing but a complexity problem. The interrelated parts combine with a randomness, and, out of that, arise real facts.

Similar to the way we take on the characteristics of someone close to us who died.

Our body keeping them alive.

When development cuts off one portion of habitat from another portion, it's called a fault line, or fault zone, so that even as the elephant habitat is shrinking in terms of its absolute size, its living space is being fragmented, migratory patterns are cut off, and interference is constant.

Michael thinks there are fault zones in New York City. On one block, you're as safe as you'll ever be, turn the corner and walk one block, and you're in a mini-war zone. This, for some reason, is how my memory works, I'll be going along, chatting to someone about something innocuous, until they say something that creates a kind of unexpected fault zone in my mind, which is what Michael did to me when he said, when he started to say, *I don't know why* . . . his hand on my back, his voice disappearing as he crossed into my mini-war zone.

"I Don't Know Why" is a Stevie Wonder song that the Rolling Stones recorded, released by ABKCO in 1975 on their album, *Metamorphosis*. Forester listened to this song as loud as his huge speakers could belt it. From where I stood at the edge of his yard overlooking Tsavo National Park, watching on the horizon the zebra and wildebeest and very occasionally a group of elephants, silhouetted in the dusk, their trunks like ribbons waving to one another across a darkening purple sky, I could hear the drums and occasional rise of Mick's voice, almost mad, almost sad, saying, *I don't know why I love you.* This feigned uncertainty, this slavery to unstoppable and irrational emotion, combined with what the song feels like, which is that you know exactly why you might love someone and know as well that you do, this play with not knowing what you know, is a vortex I spin in, while I lie naked in bed with Michael, holding back, as he says, on those nights, trying to not feel, trying to forget that I want him, want life, want to live.

During Forester's parties I would leave the house, go out to the edge of the yard, and listen to certain songs in solitude. Because when the singer or piano or guitar is speaking to you, it's better to listen alone, so that their voice is not lost in the wilderness of other people. On the far edge of the party, still able to hear the music, I would stand with my hands holding onto the free spaces in the barbed wire and wait for the faint thrust of a guitar, and the voice that was filled with enough emotion to vanquish the emptiness around me.

Just before midnight, I leave my apartment and walk to the grocery store in search of something to eat. I have wandered down each aisle at least twice, to no avail. I can never find anything to eat. The dank air reminds me of pesticides, preservatives, sickness, and death. I'm wandering the aisles of the health food section holding a bag of rice cakes, when I turn the corner and see him standing there, in front of the chocolate chips and brownie mix. He is slouching a little. My stomach surges, plummeting.

"Michael," I say.

"Hi." He's surprised. He tosses his bag of chocolate chips back on the shelf and hugs me. He doesn't hold grudges, and he never acts like I've rejected him, which my friends think is strange but I find it to be one of his more charming qualities.

"I was thinking chocolate chip cookies for dinner," he says.

"You haven't eaten yet either?"

"Nah."

He has shaved, and he's wearing the blue-green t-shirt that I like. He kisses me for several seconds on the neck. Then he picks up a box of Duncan Hines Double Fudge Brownie Mix and smells it. He finally buys a bag of chocolate chip cookies with pecans and I buy rice cakes and we drive in his truck to the airport to watch the planes land. We park behind a wire mesh fence. The night is dark and soft and the one 747 glides forever just before it lands. His windshield is cracked and I have to look either above or below the crack to watch the plane.

Michael leans back in his seat, his hands resting on his thighs. He looks like he's about to fall asleep.

"So, let me see that letter," he says.

I'm surprised he knows I've been carrying it around with me. He means the letter Forester sent. I find my wallet and extract the flimsy piece of paper. Forester writes that he is selling his land in Kenya so the government can build a landing strip. It is my last chance to see the place, if I care to. I tell Michael they'll probably build the landing strip over my mother's grave. The letter smells of the past, the impending summer, Elena's hair.

"Maybe she'll like the planes in holding patterns above her," Michael says.

I lean back, rest my feet on the dashboard.

"Maybe," I say, "but I doubt it."

Michael should know a few things—just like I do—about the impossibility of trying to get facts to line up. The first time we came to watch the planes Michael talked about how the atmosphere is a liquid—a force the plane propels against—and described the highways in the sky, set flight patterns at various altitudes. And he told me that when he was sixteen both of his parents died in South America while studying macaws. They were flying over the Amazon when they crashed into a cliff in their single engine Cessna 152 because of a "sudden deterioration in weather conditions," according to the report filed, according to the one source of information he has about exactly how they died.

Tonight he is interested in the details of Elena's death. I want to flip on the radio but it gets bad reception—the one thing I tend to hold against him—so I look for more planes.

And then his mood changes. I can feel it not even looking at him. I'm glad he's onto something other than Elena, but I am not in the same state of mind.

He crumples the cookie bag and throws it on the floor. I turn on the radio, the song barely surfacing above the grating hiss of static, and try to distract him. I know a lot about elephants.

"The elephant penis," I inform him, "weighs, on average, sixty pounds."

He makes a look like he's impressed. Then he reaches over and takes down my dress. His hands are always warm, but they are quick and know what they want. I am naked before I get the chance to get used to the idea, and the seat is scratchy and dusty.

But Michael knows how to apply himself when he wants to, and before long I focus on my white thighs in the darkness, on the sound of his voice, on his warm hands and on wanting more. But he has figured something out: he quits before I even want to let go.

"My house tonight?" he asks.

We drive back still listening to the music beneath the static. As soon as we enter, Michael's macaw, Magali, jumps down from the refrigerator and starts squawking at him.

"Relax," he tells her. "Let's see." He grabs my bag of rice cakes. "Have one of these."

I like Magali all right, but she is loud and can be aggressive. She doesn't like rice cakes all that much either, as Michael already knows, and as I walk by she follows me with one of her yellow eyes, as though trying to look right through me.

Michael lives in the basement of a house. His two roommates live in the bedrooms on the main floor. His rent is almost nothing, but there are pipes that run every which way, and fat, slow-moving cockroaches that creep along the rock walls, and an ominous looking water heater in the same section as the old boards and paint buckets. Once I stood up quickly and the top of my head hit the hardest, most unyielding pipe I have ever felt. The black finish blended in with the unfinished boards above. I thought my head would be smashed in when I touched the top of it, but it wasn't.

He has a single bed underneath the stairway, partially hidden by his clothes, which hang above it. The bed is bowl shaped, sunken in the middle, not that great for sleeping but okay for sex, and if I'm exhausted enough, from my sustained desire without release, I can sleep right up next to Michael's sweaty body and not wake up until the light.

As soon as we are down the stairs he takes off my dress again, and I love the way he touches me and the way he will stay hard forever and does anything and everything I want him to. And then it seems safe, he has taken forever and we are underneath the clothes hanging above his bed and we are laughing and then he does that one small thing, looks beyond my shoulder, and I hear the hollow shuffling sounds of the burning man, the way he unfolded the newspapers like wings, opening, collapsing, and the scream, the disembodied scream, and I squeeze my eyes shut, Michael's sweaty body pounding me until I open my eyes to see the glint of a gaze that is not in a trap; it is a gaze pointed and shattering and I don't know who he is and his breathing sounds like running, like moaning, and I am about to beg him, let me go, and then I am crying, tears mixing with sweat in the damp cool basement and then it's over. Michael doesn't ask any questions, he just tells me how great I am, so I leave it at that.

2

Michael's only window is a smeared slate of glass that faces the sidewalk. The lower half of the window is actually facing the dirt below the sidewalk. I slip out of bed and walk over to check on the black widow spider that lives in the corner, under an old Coke bottle. She usually just sits there quietly. Above the spider, on the sidewalk, I see the scissoring legs of one adult and two children, and beyond them, car tires rolling by.

Magali squawks and Michael wakes up, his eyes bloodshot, smiling at me. He moves his clothes away to look at the clock hanging from the back of his staircase.

"I have to go—Ian's already waiting," he says.

Today they are driving two hours to an uncharted canyon on an old Anasazi site. I can hear the water through the pipes and think I'll go home to shower so I don't have to deal with his roommates and the dirty bathroom.

"Take a shower with me," I say.

He is already dressing, his jeans on, his shirt half-buttoned. He squints at me.

"I don't have time."

"A five-minute shower," I say, "so I don't have to go home."

"Two minutes."

"Okay."

Afterwards, he doesn't even dry off, just struggles to pull on his jeans, which stick to his wet legs.

"Bye, babe. I'll see you this afternoon. I'm going to make Ian get back on time."

I decide to retrace yesterday's pathway exactly. I even stand at the fence and look at the African-sculpture-turned-dog-bone for a while, which is what seemed to set me off on the wrong course yesterday. It was the dog bone that made me forget my grape juice. I switch my direction toward the new Kinko's, take the narrow alley with the construction, and cross over the landscaping of the drive-thru.

The cement behind Burger King where the homeless man died is streaked with black lines, black smudges, in the very vague pattern of his moving body. I study the marks. I mentally classify them like I would a petroglyph. The directions they face, height, width, location. Could anyone read these marks as made by a man in a trap? The liquor bottles are gone but there is a shard of broken glass. Several plastic and a few wilted flowers and a stack of school papers with the headline, "Homeless Man Takes Own Life," are scattered around the spot. From the real flowers I smell a faint sweetness. I glance at the article while I stand there, which is mostly about what we can do to help the homeless, numbers to call, various soup kitchens that need volunteers. They don't mention how a girl happened to be standing nearby with a lighter in her hand, nor do they mention that the manager of Burger King stood against the wall the entire time watching as the man writhed in fire.

I take a paper. The sun is hot, bleaching the words white as I walk.

I'm late for work, but I weave into a drugstore for the cold grape juice I wanted yesterday. They don't have Welch's, so I buy an orange juice and take a new alley out, which drops me off in front of a used bookstore. It's a ratty place I've never been in, with racks of old, sun-faded books and magazines.

There is a photograph of Bob Dylan on the cover of an old *Rolling Stone* magazine in the rack. I put down my things and pick it up. I have seen Dylan's face change over the years. I have seen it become what it is. I can see him more clearly than I can Elena.

After Elena disappeared, I moved in with my father and his new wife and her kids. In the three years I lived with him, he traveled a lot and I spent most of my time in my room, listening to music. When I learned that Bob Dylan's *Blood on the Tracks* hit the charts in 1975, the year we were in Africa, I took it, even then, as a sign from Elena. It was my access to her, and I listened to the album over and over, in love with the man who wrote it, wanting for myself anyone who would feel so much emotion about me, yet all the while understanding that part of him was blind to who his lover really was. The mood of that album, with all of its pathos and romance and sarcasm, seemed to me the clue to who my mother really was. The woman in that album is a dominant and mysterious force, but she herself cannot and does not speak. For one thing, speaking wouldn't be worth it (it's all too complicated for language), and for another, the guy would just turn it around and use whatever was said for his own purposes, use her to forward and fuel his own emotions.

Way back then everything about *Blood on the Tracks* promised to take me to my mother. Dylan's music was my personal tracking device, and I used it to follow her footprints, where here and there lay the blood, sometimes still wet, which made me wonder if what I was tracking might still be alive. Occasionally, between the words of love and desire and longing, I would hear whispering, strange and inexplicable, someone saying *run* or *murder,* as the music played and the sun descended and rose again.

The light is beating down, and over the words on the magazine there is a cracked and moving pattern of black: a bird flying overhead. I step into the shade of the building and read the article. The author has varied opinions on what such and such Dylan lyric might mean. It's absurd. All opinions are absurd. No one seems to understand that Dylan is tracking something too. It will be terrible when Dylan dies. He was never blind, ever. It was Elena. It was me.

With Sam, we traveled around China right before we moved to Africa. In Red China we saw hospitals with dirt floors and no anesthesia. They don't need anesthesia, Sam would say, they have acupuncture. And at a small party, demonstrating both hypnosis and acupuncture simultaneously, Sam inserted a seven-inch needle through my mother's hand: in through her palm, out between the two middle bones on the back of her hand. I am thinking of Elena and her hand because she was willing to let go in that way, to allow Sam to hypnotize her, allow herself to feel no pain. It is true that I'm not willing to go so far with anyone, that I do hold back, as Michael says.

To let go is to pour liquor all over your newspaper cave and set it on fire. Or to record *Blood on the Tracks.*

To hold back is to stall, waiting to find out how the facts fit together.

I drop the magazine back in the rack and walk to work.

The burned man reminded me of what I used to consider a kind of secret knowledge—I used to imagine I could tell a great deal about a person with one glance in their eyes. I could evaluate their intelligence, honesty, immaturity, ability to be evil. And then I realized, it could also be found in the sound of their voice, their spirit speaking out from beneath their words and breath, another life force, darting out, diving away. And then, say, in bars, easy enough, without the eyes to look at, I could see it in the walk. There is such a thing as an intelligent walk. There is a way a child can reach the sun by just walking on the curb of a sidewalk.

Then one day I lost it—the meaning of the looks blended and became veiled. The intelligence turned into arrogance; the life force became ego; the deadness, pain; the pain, evil. When my so-called intuition ended I had trouble deciding on anything one way or another. In a way, this left me feeling more objective, and maybe more like my mother, who seemed to be able to engage in any interaction and remain unscathed. When I think of Elena, I hear the sound of her camera, clicking slow and melodious even at 250th of a second. Elena, in the end, would do anything to get her photograph. She didn't believe that news was only of passing interest; she believed that photojournalism was a road to the truth. She also, somehow, managed to believe in the objective truth of her camera. I personally don't often read the news, slanted as it is, unless there's a war, unless people are throwing themselves up against an electric fence because they cannot conceive of living another day, or unless I sense that the reporter managed to capture exactly how something really happened, the spirit that brought it to existence.

When I arrive at work I am faced with all new petroglyphs, all abstract, residing in what feels like a kind of hieroglyphic. They look like parts of words, and they make me nervous. I decide on a Snapple iced tea for lunch, and by the time I leave I feel oppressed, burdened, and jittery.

But as I walk down the alley through the shadows of the telephone lines I begin to feel better, as though by walking it will all unfold before me: clarity.

When I cross out of the alleyway and onto the sidewalk I see Michael sitting on the hood of my car. He's back exactly on time. He's occasionally sitting there waiting for me, content to just sit around like that with nothing to read or do or even look at. With the other cars and the angle I'm walking I don't notice until it's too late. There is a woman, leaning on my car, her back to him, for the most part, but she turns to look at him, saying something. I can't believe it's really her. I can't keep walking; I need to disappear. They haven't seen me yet, but I am in full view. I look behind me—there is a short cinderblock wall in the neighbor's yard, a few trees—if I could just run backwards maybe I could hide.

"Oh, hi, honey!" She waves at me, her arm an exaggerated arc, as though I can't see her, as though I'm very far away.

My heart is doing its thing: beating rapidly without actually pumping the blood. I am going to die.

I manage to move toward them.

My mother, Elena, is standing there, quite cheerful about something. She wears her hair short now, curling around her neck, and dresses with elegance, as she calls it. I call it conservative, one-color linen dresses, that kind of thing. We talk on the phone every couple of weeks. She lives on the other side of town, and she never visits without planning it about a month in advance; she is ultra-organized. So this is an arbitrary visit. Unplanned. I'm furious and shocked. I want to scream at her to get away and disappear like she did so many years ago.

"I'm so *glad* to finally meet Michael," she says.

"Yeah," I say, looking at Michael. He is a stone statue, not moving.

"It's wonderful," she continues. "So how are you?" She shades her face from the sun with her hand.

I haven't seen her in a couple of months. The light is blazing and it still isn't bright enough. If it were brighter she would disappear. I don't say anything. I can't breathe very well around her.

I've been meaning to tell Michael a few things for a long time. Like how Elena didn't actually die, I just thought she did. Or maybe even wished she did, since it would have made everything easier. Or really, the absolute truth is that I always get the feeling, every day, that my mother is about to die. The same way, when I was a kid, that I thought the world was about to end. Soon. Probably today. And then this is funny too: I never felt like she was alive. She's the kind of woman who seems untouchable. She's not good at expressing emotion. Or when she does, it seems petty. When she gets mad her voice gets high and flighty, exhibiting an immediate but small crack in her persona. She gets mad about what she considers injustices to her or anyone else's dignity. If Michael were not a statue sitting on my car I could show him this—it is easy to get her riled up. Just say something politically inappropriate.

"You taking care of yourself?" she asks.

"I'm fine. Listen," I tell her, "Michael and I . . . we have something to talk about."

"And who am I to get in your way? I'm sure you see Michael here quite a bit, and you never see your poor old mom. Let's have dinner."

"Actually," I say, pulling on Michael's arm, "it's important and urgent that I speak with Michael. But I'll come and see you soon."

Michael resists me, not budging.

"Why don't we all go to dinner?" he asks.

"Because I have to talk to you," I say.

"So, Elena tells me a lot about Africa," he says to my mother.

"Oh?" she says. "That was a long time ago."

"Yeah, but you'd think it was yesterday," he says, sliding off the hood of my Honda, not looking at me.

I'm hoping Michael won't tell her about the letter Forester wrote to her, which came to me, about three weeks or so ago.

What is the compulsion to maintain one's decorum? My mind is turning over on itself, yelling at Michael, *I'm not a liar, I'm not. You just don't understand.*

But instead we are all walking down the sunny street toward El Patio, the nearest restaurant that I more or less trust.

"Why are you here?" I ask her.

"Oh, I was just in the neighborhood," she says, breezily, like it's the most natural thing in the world.

Michael asks her questions about Africa. How long were we there? What were we doing?

As we walk, I somehow manage to blame the homeless man. It's my punishment for not helping him. Anytime there's been blood and death in my life Elena has been near.

The night I told Michael my mother was shot in Kenya while taking photos of a massacred elephant I had known him for about three days and he had a warm hand on my thigh and I felt like he knew me. And since he had just told me about how his parents died, I never went back to that moment, which I suppose is related to just standing around while a man burns to death—I let the world do its thing.

Michael has not looked at me once. I'm shaking because Elena is making everything sound different than it was. She has a way of glossing over the truth. I shouldn't be here. I'd like to take away all the events, words, looks, pauses, and desires—the entire endlessly colliding trajectory that brought me to this moment. I want out of this.

I casually lean back from the table, pretending that everything is fine, but I am about to leap over the fence and into the alleyway and attack, run, scream, or die. Be shot at, maybe, or have a heart attack.

I focus on my breathing, lean back, and lift the front two legs of the chair into the air.

"So what do you think, Elena?" my mother asks.

I think I will throw this plate to the flagstone patio. We are eating outside, under the slated shade of a portico. That will show her what socially acceptable is. She's big on that.

She excuses herself from the table to go to the restroom.

Michael is finally looking at me like he wants to say something but can't decide what to say. He leans toward me.

"I wonder now," he says, "what has been going on in your mind all this time that I didn't see."

He looks at me, and I think he wants to tear away at my flesh to see what's underneath, where my soul is. He might think I don't have one.

I want to break open my heart for him. I want him to see his face, because his face is all I care about. I want him to see what's around me—the hot asphalt streets, the water glasses with condensation on them, the blackbirds lining the telephone lines in the alley behind the fence.

"Look," I say, "it was on my mind to tell you for a long time, but I believe it myself, it seems true to me."

"You *lied*, or you're crazy. My mother and father both died, you know that, and it is not something to be joked with and it is not something you imagine for your own selfish amusement."

He stands up, which I didn't think he would do. He pulls his shirt away from his body, airing his chest. It is the usual white shirt, wrinkled and untucked, with jeans and boots.

"But I didn't mean to lie. I didn't even really know you when I first told you about her being buried in Africa. I tell everyone that. It's just something I say. It was a long time ago," I explain.

He purses his lips together, moving his mouth in a way that means he's about to explode or become indifferent, and still standing there, he drops his wrinkled money on the table from up high, so that it floats down, landing on a wet spot on his plate.

He is about to walk away.

I know a lot about Michael. I know the exact but ineffable gold-brown shade of his eyes. I know his lemon-salt smell and the low grain of his voice and the small moles and patterns of his hairs and wrinkles and the shape and feel of his rather rough mouth and his bony strong hands and his feet. I know the way he can wrap a room around himself with one slow curve of his hips when he dances and I know what will drive him to throw his fist through a door. I usually know how to make him laugh and I know how he argues for his ideas and how he travels and how his mind works in everyday life. I've spent all night talking to him as the moon crossed the sky until finally the stars lightened and the sun glowed over the mountains staining everything with long colors. I know these things from talking to him but I also know it from being quiet and letting things happen. There is a lot I don't know and maybe there is a lot I'll never know and maybe it is stuff that I could have never known or is just unknowable. There are unknowns, black boxes everywhere. It doesn't take long to figure someone out enough to start pushing their buttons, to get them to do this or that or feel this or that. But the variables could always change. Isn't it possible that one day, *for no discernable reason,* Elena could walk out of the house and never come back? Isn't that possible? I did not know that Michael would consider a little lie to be such a serious betrayal. Why didn't I know about Michael and his principles if I know so much? Why didn't I know that his mind was not the kind that leaps around between worlds?

"When you told me about your parents—" I say, "I felt that I understood—"

"You don't understand."

"But I do—"

Elena has returned.

"Where are you off to?" she asks him.

He nods at her, shakes her hand. "Nice to meet you. I've got to be somewhere," he says, and his shirt flutters out, away from his body, like an elephant ear, and back down, and he is gone.

I will run after him, explain everything. The complexity problem.

Elena is talking but the Elena I remember is still missing. And now so is Michael. I tilt my chair and take up my water, throw my head back and swallow. I lean farther onto the two back legs of my chair and feel as though I have chosen to fall into the huge space beneath the street, the darkened roach-filled underground and beyond. I fall forward in my chair, and drop to a stop. I have to get out of here. Clear and round, the glass is steady against my grip; I hold it, release it, and hold it again.

3

The strange finality in Michael's empty expression, and the sudden absence of him, is causing my entire chest, from my heart to my stomach, to collapse. I can't breathe. I'm going to suffocate. When the waiter walks over, clears dishes, and asks me a question, I can't hear what he says. Everything is silent. I watch the long rays of sun bend stealthily through the trellis above me and proceed on their way over the flagstone. I cannot move from this spot; I am a heap in the chair: my insides are hollowed out, devastated. My torso is a lump of bloody flesh.

A hyena, when shot, will rip itself apart. If the bullet lodges in his side or back, he will twist around rapidly to the pain and bite his own flesh, seizing his intestines with his teeth, pulling them out of his body, circling around himself the entire time in a mad frenzy. This is what I need to do, deconstruct everything I am to find out where the mistake is, but I will be more systematic: pull out all my guts, inspect them, change them, and put them back.

This is one mistake I make with men: I use them to help me integrate into society and the physical world. Men are so physically aggressive, whether it's splitting atoms or moving boxes or flying to the moon—they push off from the immediate physical world. I don't do this, I just see the bridges they build and the tracks they lay, rusting and crumbling in rain and sun; I see weeds breaking through concrete; the moon glowing through broken glass; the glamour they seek being washed off at night in a cracked porcelain sink—I see the untouchable spirit of the world falling, a star escaping the sky.

So when I find Michael, with a mission and a hunger, who is also ineffectual and afraid, I latch on, because he knows both worlds, the world of DNA splicing and unthinking action, and the world that is spinning away with the falling spirit of man.

The waiter returns to pour me more water. He stands around for several seconds and says something and then goes away.

I plan my escape, a silent race over highways. But when I stand, the world takes a long time to navigate, and as I push my chair away from the table with my legs, the chair falls over backwards. Finally a sound, metal crashing on flagstone.

It is difficult to walk out to the sidewalk.

Sun rays glide over my feet, and I imagine following them to Africa. I will find a hyena and pull the trigger myself, to better understand the pain. With this as a plan, I can almost breathe. And then a real plan, the obvious plan, occurs to me—I will go to Africa to get my mother's body before they build the landing strip. This feels so right; it feels true. And the collapsed body I'm in takes me more quickly down the sidewalk.

I've been told I'm a stubborn person, not inclined to change my mind once I've decided on something. So if I decide, at the age of nine, that my mother is dead, seeing her live her life after the accident, and talking to her maybe every couple of weeks, is not really enough to make me change my mind. I gather facts around Elena like Elena gathered photographs, and perhaps for the same reason, because I believe that the evidence will add up to something if I can figure out how to put it together—like a type of Rubik's Cube—if you put all the squares together, you can see the image. I see her image only in her ending. It gathers around her.

At the end of the second street, I walk inside a dank grocery store and stand in line for a long time. I flip through *Vogue* to distract myself, looking at a special section devoted to red lips, red hair, red clothes, red underwear, and I scan all the headlines on the gossip newspapers. Finally, I trade in a ten for a roll of quarters and walk outside. I lean against the ice machine, which is surprisingly warm, and slip my quarters into the pay phone. It takes forever to get through to information, but they dial the Kenyan embassy in Washington for me, which has only a long recording stating the address of the Kenyan Consulates General in New York City, which I memorize because I don't have a pen. Visas take two or three days and cost thirty dollars.

As I talk to the lady at the New Mexico Department of Health I am tempted to tell her that elephants communicate with infrasound—long sound waves that travel easily, bending over and around obstacles—because she is telling me, over phone lines that might as well be long sound waves, as she taps out the information I requested and waits for it to come up on her computer screen, that if only she could tell her husband to be careful today, with the drive-by shootings and all, she would feel better. If only she knew infrasound, I think, like an elephant, so that he could hear her as he drives away.

Michael, I can already hear his sarcasm, would say, why doesn't she just get a cell phone, use the radio waves, like any normal person?

I watch the traffic in the heat, watch a few cars pull into Ron's El Camino Real for the real thing, red chile that leaves your mouth burning.

The lady at the Department of Health is looking up for me the requirements for yellow fever and cholera and hepatitis A and B shots, and the recent incidence of Rift Valley Fever. The shots, she finally says, are strongly recommended but not required—as long as I enter Nairobi from America. I've been reading lately about the various side effects of vaccines, worse sometimes, than the disease. Not that I usually disregard science altogether, but lately I have come to realize that so much of research is in the name of profits and money, and conditional to those, like everything else.

An obnoxious kid who is not quite still a kid is whipping around on a short bicycle in the parking lot right in front of me. He has almost gotten himself killed at least three times, though I think he's oblivious to this fact.

There is a peso or something stuck in the phone beside me and someone is waiting for my phone, but I dial Michael's number anyway. He doesn't answer and I don't say anything, but on his machine I let him listen to the traffic in the parking lot and the kid on his bike yelling to another kid on a skateboard. I wonder if he can interpret these sounds, if he'll know they're from me.

I walk back to my apartment and start packing. No one in their right mind leaves town because of getting caught at some lie they told, I know that, but I'm on my way out, and tonight too, because if I don't go now when will I ever go? And if I'm not invulnerable now, when will I ever be?

I realize with some surprise that I care nothing about most things in my apartment. I care about Michael, maybe that's the only thing in my life. I have a few things that make me feel all right, like one photo that Elena took in Africa, an old ring of hers, and a few of Michael's t-shirts. I take these and stuff them with dresses, tank tops, jeans, shoes, and a few sweaters into a duffel bag. I double-check to make sure I have my two credit cards, then I haul my bag with a couple of blankets and a pillow all out to my car.

I sit for a while, looking at a road atlas. Then I cruise around town looking for Michael's old turquoise truck, but it's not on any of the streets near his house.

I drive an old white Honda with a blue stripe. I call it Angel because I can cruise the local streets at sixty and no one ever stops me; I'm invisible; an angel flying through town on a heat wave. The light bends over my car so that as I glide through traffic, I am only a blur of light. As I accelerate around the corner of the dirt alley, blackbirds fly up out of trees and cross the sky over Godfather's Pizza. It is almost dark.

I reach behind the passenger seat to the three hundred or so tapes in a box beneath a pillow and pull out Beethoven's *Appassionata*.

I stop to get gas. I add a quart of oil to the engine and check the air in the tires. Behind the gas station I change into one of Michael's t-shirts, and then I am driving away from it all.

I drive recklessly, taking the thin dark highways to the north at ninety-five miles per hour. I practice driving without headlights, switching off the white beams and accelerating steadily into blackness. I feel the trees passing, thick with weight, perfect in their isolation. Dim green from the radio is the only illumination on my hands until finally the blackness grows elaborate webs and I hurriedly take my glowing fingers and flip the lights, high beams suddenly flooding the tunnel of darkness ahead.

On a switchbacked road, north on Highway 64 toward Raton, it is raining so violently that I can't see anything except the lightning turning the trees before me into ghosts. I feel a quiet thrill with the weather—it is unrelenting, dangerous. I dare myself to drive faster, into the streaking darkness. What does it take to get struck? Is that the kind of thing one can plan? The rain on the hood of my car taps violently. *Run,* my mother told me. It took me this long to take her advice; I should have ran years ago.

Finally, there is a local gas station to my left, but the whole parking area is a small lake. I pull in anyway, and park in the water. Perhaps the lightning will strike and my tires will transmit the electricity to the car doors. I'm thinking about running into the store, to buy some water or something, when the electricity goes out, leaving the whole parking lot black and beaten with rain.

I am afraid, of what I don't know, but I lock my doors and wrap myself in a blanket.

The next morning I wake to a sunny gas station parking lot, though I'm still parked in several inches of water. Tree branches have fallen here and there. It's hot, and I change into a pair of shorts and sandals and an old polka-dotted bathing suit top. I call my boss and tell her I'm looking for petroglyphs, and that I need a leave of absence.

In southern Colorado I suffer a three-hour delay because of some roadblock set up to catch a guy suspected of killing a cop.

They have traffic backed up for seven miles in both directions so I turn off onto a reservation. I stop and park on the side of the road and watch a black-haired boy on a horse herding sheep through a field of grass. The boy is wearing a loose red shirt that whips in the wind, and the sheep blend in so well to the tall sun-bleached grass that I see them only when they are moving. The endless land is divided by the road I am on, and the sky is unbroken above me.

In Kansas the rain falls in sheets, a curtain daring me to part it. And as I do the road dries suddenly, hot with sun. The land is flat then, and my mind with it, coasting forward evenly and without concern.

I am a lone car at the edge of a plain.

There are no other cars on the road.

I am almost out of gas.

But I have escaped, am somehow far from it all, until I look across the vast golden plain and remember that I have seen elephants in grass almost like this, the smaller ones following their mothers. Their ears were flat against their heads for a while, and then swayed open, flapping. When the Land Rover first frightened them I saw into one young face. It held the blood-brown color of the wet dirt around us, and passed by me with a wild look.

I start sending Michael a postcard every time I stop for gas. Since he likes gas stations and worked at one when he was fourteen, I send him a photo of Richard Gere in a car garage. I also find a photo of an old Esso station in Kansas with a girl in spiked heels filling a tank. But mostly I send him half-decent shots of landscapes, sunrises, that kind of thing. Usually I try to tape a feather or toll ticket stub or part of a soft drink wrapper to the card so that he can know what I am doing in the real world, and I write to him about how the rain sounds like his uneven heartbeat and how I still haven't seen a cypress tree.

In Missouri, at the Mississippi River, there is a turtle crossing the road. I pick it up, a small box turtle, and place it in the grass at the side of the road. It doesn't even pull in its head when I pick it up, just starts off again once I put it down. I stand looking at the quickly moving river, the dividing line between east and west, a creamy coffee color with several whirling eddies. It seems to me the same color as the Niger River in Mali, but no one is washing their clothes, and right behind me a railroad track follows along instead of a dirt road.

I call Michael. He doesn't answer, so I leave a message. I tell him that Angel stalls at the red lights in each new town. I tell him there is a tapping, clicking sound in the alternator that sounds like a camera shutter, taking snapshot after snapshot, or like a telephone ringing or like someone knocking on my door, an omniscient sound, everywhere I turn. Listen. I tell Michael. Do you hear me. Do you hear my voice. The tapping is like God tapping on my door, like a heart beating, waiting.

I am buying my breakfast at a drugstore—a big bottle of orange juice and a cup of plain yogurt—when I see a poster about Dylan playing in Minneapolis tomorrow. I spoon the yogurt into the juice and shake the jar for several minutes while I walk over to the pay phone on the edge of the parking lot. I call the ticket number and I'm told that the stadium holds 10,000, and there are many tickets left. I give them my credit card number. It seems like a minor diversion.

I drive northwest instead of east. I see a dead raccoon curled on the road, looking like a baby sleeping. Every time I stop for gas the mosquitoes swarm.

I call Michael. His message machine answers, so I tell him that usually I see a whole corpse, sagging on the side of the road, but today I saw a fox tail, and then the fox's head on the yellow line. At least I think it was a fox, a bushy tail, an orange face.

I stop at a gas station for Gumout to spray into the carburetor, but they happen to be out. I tell the checkout guy about the fox.

"That ain't nothing," this guy behind me in line says. He has dark oily hair and a red t-shirt that says SCRAM.

"Once I saw a truck jump the center median and land on a van. The whole family died. And that ain't nothing neither, compared to what else I seen."

The cashier nods. "It's weird out there."

"Weird ain't the word for it," the SCRAM guy says. "It's *The X-Files* out there. I'm telling you. You can't imagine."

I need a TV. I've never seen *The X-Files*. I suddenly want to see *The X-Files*.

Back in the car I feel like a sick animal trying to get somewhere, the landscape of my mind intersecting with the criss-crossing highways and the speeding vehicles buzzing in every possible direction.

I call Michael at two in the morning, four in the morning, six in the morning. I walk around my car, around and around it.

Angel dies in a small town in the middle of an intersection. I get out barefoot and push Angel to the curb. I rummage around for the last of my Gumout to spray into the carburetor.

"Where can I buy more Gumout?" I ask a guy who is standing on the sidewalk looking at me. His t-shirt and jeans are covered in a thin sheath of mud.

"I can help you. I fix cars," he says.

"Yeah. Where can I buy more Gumout?" I ask again, but his grape-green eyes shift to the sidewalk and he tells me he can give me a lift.

"It's all right," I tell him.

He smiles and leans onto my car. "I know someplace you want to go," he says.

I spray the very last of the Gumout into the carburetor and slam down the hood.

There are large birds swirling in the sky just beyond a church steeple.

"What are those birds?" I ask.

"That's the dump," he says. "It's a great place. Wanna go?"

He is standing close enough so that I can smell his car-oil smell and menthol breath. I am wearing my usual outfit of a bathing suit top and shorts and he looks at my chest as he runs his fingers up the hood of my car. I stand there and wonder where Michael is and why he won't answer his phone. I wonder if he's dead or hurt or if his bird got hurt.

"That's my pickup." The guy points across the street to an orange, mud-splattered truck.

I like his truck. It reminds me of Michael. I like his t-shirt too, a soft smudged blue.

"I love dumps." I finally say. "I'll follow you in my car."

There is a moment of hesitation. His grip on my car tightens.

"Great," he finally says.

I get in my car, still barefoot, the road hot and burning my feet. My car starts.

"Hey," he places his hands on my car door, then traces them around the perimeter of the window. He manages to do this even while half of his body is inside my car, his head as close to mine as it can be without actually touching me. He grins, "Hey, my place is a dump too. You wanna go there?"

I quickly imagine his filthy bed and twisted sheets and sweaty, taut body. I imagine letting go of all my ideals that never got me anywhere.

"Not really," I answer.

"Or listen," he says. "I have an extra ticket. Wanna go to the Dylan concert tonight? It's in Minneapolis—about a forty-five-minute drive."

His face is too close to mine. I decide innocence is my best option.

"*Who?*" I ask.

"*Dylan.* Tonight. *Bob Dylan.*"

I shrug. "Never heard of him."

He twists around rather violently and backs out of my window, while still leaning hard on the windowsill, his chest jutting at me.

"*Jesus Christ.* Where you been? How can anyone—?" Then he starts shaking his head and is finally just standing beside my car, his arms at his side.

I want to laugh or cry, I don't know which. I know what the real world is, but in my world Dylan wrote about Elena who died in 1975, and his records exist for me alone.

"So are we going to the dump or what?" I ask.

"Oh yeah," he says, "*Jesus.*"

He walks to his car and I am safe again, in Angel, where the cheap metal and warm wind shelters me. I follow him for a while, and then I turn off onto some side road. I am heading east again. I know because the sun is behind me. I do not see him in my rearview mirror. The gas pedal is a grainy hard plastic beneath my bare foot, and as I drive a little faster, the hot summer hours are again my only companion, each one the annotation of another.

The concert is in a gray steel dome. The opening band looks like a few ants from where I'm sitting. When I try for a better view, I become one of a mass of moving bodies down to the bottom floor. I'm a little afraid of randomly running into the guy who wanted me to go with him to the dump, and the sound is bad and the experience impersonal. I push my way out before Dylan even shows up on stage, and go sit in my car in the parking lot and listen to Dylan and Johnny Cash sing "Girl From the North Country." I wonder if my mother ever considered herself to be a girl from the North Country. She was born in St. Paul. What I feel like doing is driving further north, as far north as I can, into the whiteness, but instead I stay with my plan and drive east.

The land transforms into curving ivy vines that wash over telephone poles and whip over broken lines.

For five hours I am stuck in Chicago traffic. For three hours I am behind the same car: a repainted chrome-colored Ford that plays a funk radio station so loud the entire time that his car shakes and my own music can't drown it out.

The highways in Chicago make me think that someday they will build a road around the world. It will begin in New York City, an elevated road high in the sky with ramps onto the interstates. When they get to San Francisco they will continue across the Pacific Ocean with a wide road that floats, wide enough to withstand and float over the waves. There will be huge floating stations where you stop to refuel and shop at plastic floating mini-malls. The floating highway will land in Tokyo, then cross in elevated fashion to China, where it will span through Istanbul, Tunis, Madrid, and float back to New York.

I pull over an hour later, into a gas station, and I don't see the road, or rain, or gas pumps gleaming in the lights; I see that the clouds are patterned after Elena's dresses, willowy, billowing as she turns.

That night, tremulously cruising at eighty-five up the small slope of a hill, Angel dies, the tapping ceases, and we coast to fifty, then thirty-five. I pull over to the shoulder and sit silently in the dark. As each car passes by they create a moment of vacuum space, so that I feel like a single electron in a covalent bond; our electrons merge so there is no space between us, we are one. Then they pass and I am alone again, in the silence, in Angel, wondering why I never bought more Gumout.

After a while Angel starts again, and at two in the morning, Ohio time, I call Michael. His machine picks up. Michael, Michael, Michael, I breathe into his phone until finally the machine hangs up on me.

Fragments of animals lie along the roads.

I imagine Michael crossing the street, a car slamming him to the pavement, his body flopping over, his head smashed between two cars. The panic twists the back of my neck and shoots down my spine and into my legs.

I sit awake all night in a rest stop, unable to drive, unable to sleep.

The next day I stop at a campground just outside of Cleveland that has toilets which flush, showers, sinks, and a telephone. And too many mosquitoes.

I wash my hair in the bathroom, but I forgot a towel, so I'm swinging my hair back and forth to dry it and at the same time smoothing toothpaste on my toothbrush.

A girl enters, her black hair straight up in long spikes.

"Watch it," she says.

I figure she's talking about shaking my hair, so I stop.

"Watch it," she repeats.

"Watch what?" I ask, annoyed.

"What toothpaste are you using? I was using Preparation H the other day. Some trickster put it in my bag. My teeth were oily for hours and I couldn't taste anything."

I hold my tube of toothpaste up so she can see it.

"Oh," she nods. "You going to Andrew's?"

"Who's that?"

She stretches her lips and applies a bruise-colored lipstick.

"It's a club. Where are you going?" She sprays her hair, making the tips of each black spike pointy and shiny.

"Great hairspray," I say.

"It's the best. We put flyers up with it."

I stand beside her in the mirror as she firms up her spikes. There are several of them, in one long line down the center of her head.

"Where are you going?" she asks again.

"Nowhere. I feel nauseous."

"Maybe you're pregnant."

"I doubt it."

"Anyway," she continues, "I feel nauseous too. I need to escape my boyfriend. Can I change shirts with you?"

"What?"

"I need to look different. You could too. You could walk out of this bathroom completely different."

She immediately pushes her hand into her bag and deposits into the sink makeup, more hairspray, bottles of pills, and then she holds up a long silver razor.

"Let me cut your hair. Not like mine, don't worry. Your hair is too long. That's so old-fashioned."

I glance at the razor, but I'm mostly taking in her face. She has very high cheekbones and a full, crooked mouth. From some angles she is mysterious and beautiful, and from others, doughy and monstrous. Her face has something in it that I can't look away from.

I usually just cut my own hair. I hate the smell in salons. I hate sitting there thinking that a haircut will change anything because it never does.

"Well," I say.

She sticks her cigarette in her mouth and turns to me.

"I'll cut your hair, shag it out, and you can come to Andrew's," she says. "Andrew's will help you forget that you're pregnant."

I'm exhausted from not sleeping the night before. I pick up the bottle of yellow pills she dropped into the sink. The label is ripped off.

She pulls a bottle of Diet Coke from her bag.

"Gimme two of those," she says. I hand her the bottle. She swallows two with her Coke and hands me two. Then she hands me the bottle.

"You can cut my hair," I say, placing the Coke in the sink and pocketing the pills.

"Really?" she says. "Oh, this is going to be great."

She starts in the back and saws at my hair, the razor seemingly less efficient than a pair of scissors would be. I immediately regret my decision, the cutting is painful and strange, but I tell myself that this isn't really about a haircut, though I see my hair falling to the floor. This is about something else.

Soon the floor is covered with hair, long strands of light folding around our feet. She, in very choppy fashion, has curved my hair to follow my jaw, shorter in the back and long in the front.

"I've always wanted this haircut," she says.

I part it on the side and push it back with my fingers and try to forget about it.

"Now you need a new shirt," she says, running her fingers along the bottom of my tight velvet green tank top, and along the top of my jeans, still wet from washing my hair in the sink.

And then she is standing topless in front of me and lifting off my shirt. She leaves my bathing suit top on, and starts pulling her torn sweaty t-shirt over my head. Her tits are brushing up against mine.

I don't want her sweaty shirt, which smells of stale coffee and cigarettes, but I'm looking into her eyes, which look almost black because her pupils are so large, and I see a rim of blue. She usually has blue eyes. A blackbird close up in the sky, and I know why I let her cut my hair. Because this girl is in a trap.

"There," she says. She has stepped into my shirt and is twisting it up her body to avoid messing up her hair. I'm worried she's stretching it.

"I want your vest," I say.

I take off her smelly t-shirt and throw it in the trash. She looks into the trash can for a few seconds.

"Okay," she shrugs. "He bought it for me."

"I need some kind of shirt besides that white t-shirt," I say.

"Put on the vest. It will make you look tough."

I put on the vest, which is heavy and maybe a little damp and a tight black leather. I look in the mirror. I'm looking at her more than at myself and I get the distinct feeling that she will die tonight, and since this is an illogical thing to think, I think that she is the sign that I will die tonight, and then I stop thinking all together.

"Well, I gotta go." She looks in the mirror and then at me. "Do I look sexy like you did? Green goes with spikes, right? But do I still look tough?"

"Yeah," I say. I miss my shirt.

"You look tough now," she says, "much more than before. Come with me to Andrew's," she says. "Andrew's will help you forget that you're pregnant."

"I'm probably not pregnant."

"From your expression, girl, you are. Don't worry, I've had two abortions. It's not so bad. Have you had one?"

I can now hear the rapid heartbeat of a baby.

"No," I say.

"Well, I gotta go." She looks in the mirror and then at me. "I'm going to spray your hair."

She holds up what is left of my hair and sprays it straight up, so that I'm reminded of someone who is concerned with achieving the impossible, the unreachable. My hair is abstract.

"I'll see you," she says, and I watch her shoulder blades move in her back as she walks away and out the door.

I avoid looking in the mirror and decide to leave the camp-ground and drive all night. A cop immediately pulls me over for driving sixty-five. I tell him I'm from out of town.

"Yes, I can see that. Here in Ohio, we're a strict fifty-five," he says.

"Okay. I'm sorry, sir."

"So—I'll let you off." He taps the top of his hat and swaggers back to his car.

When I am out of Ohio I drive blindly.

I listen to the clicking of the alternator, thumping like the heart-beat of a baby.

The humidity is warm and thick but there is a wind through the windows. I look down to see myself doing ninety. A white cross stands on the side of the road, and yet the road is flat, only slightly curvy. I try to imagine how much worse it would be in winter.

If it all ended right here for me, no one would know to put up two little white crosses, instead of one. I pull over on the side of the highway just a few feet beyond the flower-covered cross where someone died. Everyone says that some things will change you—there is a turning point in which you are not the same person you once were. I am afraid nothing will change me. I am afraid that no matter how I change what I do, I cannot change my fate. I do not know my fate; I just know that it feels out of my control.

When the sun rises, I drive to a gas station. The leaves shimmer in the cool breeze. It is two hours earlier in Albuquerque. I call Michael.

A sweet, clear voice answers, a girl.

The space between my heart and my stomach collapses, this

time completely. Michael, even with two roommates, has his own phone. His own answering machine.

"Is Michael there?" I ask.

"Ummmm," she says, eating something as she talks. "He's in New York."

"New York? What's he doing there?"

"I don't know," she slurs. "Hold on—I have to take out my retainer. I don't know. I'm visiting his bird while he's gone, who happens to hate me, by the way. She's sleeping upstairs tonight. I don't usually spend the night but I'm in a fight with my roommate."

"Oh. Try raisins," I say.

"Raisins?"

"Yeah, the yellow kind. For Magali, they have to be yellow."

"She might bite me."

"Just lay the raisins out, and talk to her in a normal voice. Don't take it personally, she's temperamental."

"Okay," she says, "okay."

"So, about Michael," I say.

"Oh right. He gave me his brother's phone number. . . . What time is it? I don't know where . . . hold on."

"It's early," I say. "Sorry about that. Michael doesn't care about that kind of thing."

"I was asleep. Oh, here it is. Here's the number."

"Thanks," I say.

I can breathe. The air is sweet with damp leaves and the dawn is turning the highways pink, and I am driving toward Michael who is waiting for me in New York, anticipating that I am on my way to Africa.

I call Michael's brother. There is no answer. I pull over to the side of the road and without meaning to, I fall asleep.

A few hours later I call again. The phone rings several times before he answers, a close voice, a feigned laziness, like I woke him up, like he knew I would call. Michael's younger brother, Trey. With the same lilting accent, rough voice.

"I'm looking for Michael," I tell him.

I hear a long exhalation.

I pause. "Sorry to bother you."

"No bother."

I hear a woman's voice in the background. I don't hear the words, but the intonation of *who is it?*

"Is he in New York?" I ask.

"Yeah, he's in New York."

"Is he waiting for me?"

"Uh. I don't know." Another long exhalation. "This is Elena?"

"Yeah. I'm at a Mobil station. North of New York somewhere."

Another sigh, "Okay. I'm at 59th and 1st Avenue. East Side. By FDR Drive. You know the city?"

"No."

"Well remember East Side on 59th. It's easy. There's a big bridge."

"Okay."

"All right," he says.

I follow the signs to New York City, to the George Washington Bridge. I can feel my tires compress the oblique road until I adjust my speed to the quickness of the cars around me.

I get off the Henry Hudson and I'm supposed to be heading east. It takes me an hour to get halfway across town, but by then

I've figured out the driving rules—when there's an empty space, fill it immediately or get honked at.

I'm on Lexington Avenue, a one-way street going the wrong direction, and when I get stuck in traffic near a Duane Reade drugstore, I pull over into a bus lane, turn on my hazard lights, and jump out.

The store is cold and humid. I shiver. A cop stands in the doorway. I'm still wearing the girl's leather vest over my polka-dotted bathing suit top and my shorts, and a few people stare. I scan past all the faces on the hair dye boxes and walk past the shampoos and tampons and cold medicines and finally find the pregnancy tests. I pick one that looks friendly and effective. It must be eighty degrees outside and humid, but the woman in front of me in line is wearing nylons and a suit jacket and her hair is stuck to the sweat on the back of her neck. It takes a long time to pay.

On my way to the car, moving downtown, I glance to my left. About twelve elephants are forging an uneven path, thick legs following their trunks, an arid savage light behind them. They are a spectral image, poorly represented on a television, a faded finite box; but there they are, wild and methodical, following each other in disjointed lines walking the same direction as me down the street.

I watch them for several seconds until they are gone, replaced by a blank screen that is indistinguishable from the computer screens, video cameras, and other things the store sells.

But the orange landscape that filtered the wild and dusky light, its waste, its wanton and ruthless unceasing airlessness, is now all around me, the voices circling, foreign and urgent.

I start walking. I get back in my car and turn off the hazard lights.

The elephants are right here, and the screeching brakes and honking horns and voices are all a kind of music, trapping me in their beat, in the rhythm of my breath.

And this is another thing that happened to me after I fell in love with Michael: I felt trapped. Not that I had ended up with the wrong person, but that love had turned into a strange desire for more, a desire for everlasting life, so that what we have can last forever, so that I can be with him always.

4

Inspired by the lovely mess of hundreds of other outfits all around me, I change into a sundress and heeled sandals and apply lipstick, a lot of it, as that seems to be the thing in this town.

I park on the corner of 58th Street looking toward 1st Avenue. I get out of my car and walk around the block to Trey's apartment building.

The entry hall ceiling is falling down, yellow water dripping into a puddle in front of the mailboxes. I have to cram myself against the door to keep from being dripped on. I half hope he won't be there, but without questioning who I am, he buzzes me up.

I walk up six flights of stairs and down a long, narrow hallway made of tin tiles painted in dull peach. Led Zeppelin's "Kashmir" reverberates off the walls. The apartment door isn't completely closed. I knock.

"Enter," he yells.

Trey is lying on a futon in the kitchen, his head hanging off the end, his eyes open and looking at me, a half-empty bottle of Jack Daniels propped on his stomach.

"Whoareyou?" he asks.

"Come in and close the door, please, I'm stuck," a female voice clips. I take one step forward and close the door. "Plus, I can't stand the music," she says. "It's the guys across the hall." She puts her hands on her hips and saunters over to Trey, threatening to drop her ice water on his stomach. "It's what—the third time they've played it now?"

"Is Michael anywhere?" I ask.

Trey sits up. "So, you're Elena. Took you a long time to get here."

He holds out the bottle of J.D. to me, nodding to it, like I need some.

"Michael drove it straight through," the girl says. "When he first got here, he slept for like, two days straight."

I walk over and take a swig. The whiskey is hot in my throat and I feel like I'll be sick if I move, so I just stand there, next to the futon, close enough to feel the heat of Trey's body. I look vaguely above his head to the top of his refrigerator, which is short and dusty, not quite as tall as me.

"There's a weird smell in here," I tell them.

"Dead mouse," the girl says. "We can't find it; I think it's behind the wall."

"Elena," Trey says my name again, as though it means something. "It might be a dead rat."

"Nice," I say.

"Yeah," he sighs, and lies back down, repositioning the bottle of liquor so that it is settled again between his hipbones on his stomach.

"We're celebrating," the girl says. "My name's Allison."

"What are you celebrating?"

"Nothing," Trey interrupts.

"Just," Allison tosses her hair, "the fact that Trey is now *rich.*"

I take the bottle out of his hands again and take another swig.

I look around his apartment, "This place is almost as bad as Michael's. Are you going to move?"

Trey glances at me. He has a rougher look than Michael; he's a little more odd, a little more familiar. I can tell he's the kind of guy who isn't quite present, thinking always about something else, something that's not happening in the room. He's looking at me longer than I think he should be, trying to figure something out, so I start looking back, thinking that he's probably sleeping around with someone other than Allison.

"No," he finally says, "why should I spend more?"

"Aren't you going to ask how he got rich?" Allison asks me.

"How?"

"*Well*," Allison says, laying her hands flat against her chest, as though over her heart, "by selling *five* paintings, *three* of which were of *me*."

"Where'd you park?" Trey asks.

"58th Street."

He nods. "Good."

"Trey's electricity is off," Allison says, "but he doesn't have a TV or a computer or an answering machine or anything else so it doesn't matter much. He reads by candlelight."

"A traditionalist," I say. "I understand, I don't have a phone."

"Perpetually broke," Allison interrupts, "until today. Or yesterday. How do you count it? The opening was last night."

I can hear it again, "Kashmir."

"Are they really going to keep playing that song?" I ask.

"As a matter of fact—" Trey says.

"Probably," Allison finishes, "over and over. And the girl below plays disco, which, weirdly, is just as annoying. Isn't it baby? I think we should move. To Tribeca, or Soho, or the Lower East Side, what do you think?"

"Can I use your bathroom?" I ask.

"It's in the back." Allison points.

I walk through the apartment. The bathroom is made up of awkward triangle shapes, but light falls into the two windows from between the buildings and reflects off the blue tiles so that I feel like I'm in a forest.

I read the instructions on the pregnancy test. I look in the mirror at the circles under my eyes. There is blue everywhere.

In the rain forests of Central Africa, the pygmies can distinguish in detail anything within thirty feet. Their eyes are trained to differentiate between snakes and leaves of the exact same shade of green, equipped to find a small patch of gray between leaves, signifying an elephant. But take a pygmy out to the savannah to see elephants thousands of yards in the distance, and he describes them as very tiny elephants, a short way off.

What one sees is determined in part by what one knows to be true, so I am careful about what I think I see. If I change what I know, I can change what I see.

I watch the control line on the pregnancy test show up and I read the instructions again to make sure which line is the control line. It is glowing pink.

I think about those pygmies and how their perception skills outside of their world failed them, because to imagine that a 6,000 to 12,000 pound elephant is close up but very tiny is to lack experience in circumventing flat distance and space. And so it must also be that certain people cannot navigate outside of their emotions and training—so that when I tell Michael my mother is dead, he thinks I purposely deceived him, purposely lied—when in fact I was only telling it the way it was for me, not for the world, since we were talking about me and not some detached fact—like you can't walk through a wall or escape gravity. There are other kinds of facts, intuitive facts, like it's good to be pregnant with a man you love, rather than someone else.

I find most people are too literal-minded. They interpret everything at face value. Or, if they are looking out for hidden meaning, so not to be tricked, they turn even that which is supposed to be literal inside out—making it more complex than it is—thereby deceiving themselves.

I think about whether or not Michael has been in this bathroom, taking a shower or looking in the mirror, and what he thinks of his brother who he never talks about. It's a huge bathroom, almost half as big as the bedroom I just walked though. I can hear pigeons—they are purring, cooing low and heavy in their throats—and "Kashmir" feels far away, so I feel better.

I look at the test and then I look at the instructions again. There is still only a control line; the test is negative. I feel relief and also shattered, like I've lost something, like when I was at El Patio and Michael walked away. I lean against the wall for a few minutes; I even turn and place my cheek against its coolness, and then I move out of the blue triangular forest and walk back to the kitchen.

Trey is still lying on the futon.

"I'm going for a walk or something," I say.

"Okay." Allison nods.

I walk past them, through the pounding bass of "Kashmir," and down the six flights of stairs.

In my car I feel like I've forgotten everything I've ever known. I look at a gash in the passenger seat and wonder how it got there. When I look up, a man and woman are crossing 1st Avenue. They are wrapped around each other as they walk, looking more like a gnarled tree than two human beings. She has long dark hair, and he's in a suit. Maybe it's the strange discontinuity of the suit, and the way the guy is waving one hand to demonstrate something he is saying while wrapped around the girl, that strikes me as odd.

It seems impossible but I'm certain it's Michael. I feel naked and foolish but I get out of the car anyway, and follow them.

They keep walking to the end of the block and around the corner.

He is animated, discussing something, his hand on the small of her back as she opens the door. I rush up quickly, skip forward, trip on a crack in the sidewalk but recover, the side of his face covered partly in shadow, she just inside the gray door, so that he is left standing there, for a moment, just before me.

"Oh," I say, too surprised to say anything else, still disbelieving.

The ultimate deception, more than anything, to see Michael in a suit. And his hair is slicked back, like in a fifties movie. It can't be him and yet it is. A suit—when in Albuquerque he wears only faded jeans and untucked button-down shirts and lives in a roach-infested basement. Who wears a suit?

I think I might faint, from not eating and not sleeping and from him, standing there, a man I've loved and never known. I feel the yellow waste of the city as it ricochets from across the street. I am hidden now, in yellow, below the unmoving sky ripped by tall towers.

I can see the girl's bright eyes from beyond the door.

"What is it?" she asks him.

"A friend of mine," he says, still looking at me, not looking at her.

I must have made a mistake; Michael looking so different than how I know him isn't Michael. I feel alone, as though I am the only one on the street, in the city, the rushing cars simply a background for my aloneness.

And now I know why Michael reminds me of my mother. Because I am here in a yellow wasteland and my world has ended. He did the same thing to me that she did.

He moves toward me, a few feet, his back straight and hips slouched, carrying his appearance into the void around me, so that it is all enough to stop me altogether. I turn around and walk to the curb.

He follows and circles me, moving from the sidewalk to the street and again to the sidewalk. His eyes look dark and he smells like whiskey.

"Your tan seems to be fading." He smiles, stepping around me, making me pause.

I don't really tan so I don't know what he's talking about. He smells like he is sweating alcohol, which mixes with the heat and musky air and swirls through my throat.

He takes off his jacket.

"It's hot," he says, still just standing there.

The girl is still in the doorway, and Michael's shirt is damp and shines with the yellow setting sun, a liquid fire, a memory. I have felt heat like this, felt the sweat break out on my own body, watching the elephants, watching the dust rise as they walked.

Michael seems slightly thinner, slightly more pale.

He is speaking, but his voice is suspended in air so that I can hear each word but not what he's saying. It is partly the traffic; I hear the words *don't* and *know*, but there is more traffic than words, and mostly he is looking at me like he wants to say something else. A look I've seen before. He is standing close.

"I told the girl at your house to feed Magali yellow raisins," I finally say, quietly.

He looks at me, narrowing his eyes to slits, then he laughs.

"It's good to see you," he says, "considering I—your hair—"

"I'm sorry about—"

"Michael?" The girl is standing beside us now, except she's on the curb and we're in the street. She has perfect hair and red lips.

"What's going on?"

He looks from the sidewalk to me to her, back and forth, with even timing, like a second hand, ticking.

She is a lanky version of Ava Gardner. Very pretty, expensively dressed.

"Why are you so drunk?" I ask, but it comes out as a whisper.

"Ahhh," he says. His eyes are almost as red as Elena's used to be, drunk-red and muddy brown, a river running with blood.

"I—don't—know—why—" his finger points to invisible sections of air and lands on me with the word "why."

People are walking down the sidewalk beside us and their voices rise above the rush of cars in the background, each new voice superseding the next. My body fills with heat, with violence and despair. A rollerblader passes by and I smell dog shit and car exhaust through the continuum of cars, and I think about how Michael and I were eating cinnamon buns in the parking lot of the Frontier

Restaurant in Albuquerque and how he was talking to me about recapturing the past, which is what I'd like to do now, go back to that moment, knowing now as much as I ever did that that was the moment that would define all others. Each moment defines the next except at some point it's too late to turn around.

He looks at me slow and intense and walks all the way around me and to the street again. He places his hand on my back, his fingertips spread out like a spider, and holds them there a while, until it feels like several hands.

As I walked through the market in Timbuktu, there was a sudden commotion, and all the children called rapidly to one another, running up to me, so that soon there were several hands in my hair, on my back, words in my ears. They had never seen blonde hair before. The market was made up of, had risen out of, sand, and as we walked, hundreds of flies buzzed up and resettled on dried fish. Overwhelmed and uncertain, I didn't run or try to escape, but I made myself vanish: I became the transparent desert, absorbing the weight of light, gathering the heat to my surface.

And with Michael's fingers on my back, I am the random voices around me, the yellow dusky light and car exhaust, dissipating into the endless atmosphere.

He is afraid; I can hear it in his breathing.

Or maybe I am afraid.

I see him shield his eyes from the sun, remembering a woman he loved, and her inability to know what that meant.

The air is thick, smothering, and before I know it, I am running, faster than I ran across the dunes away from my mother, so fast that I am sprinting around the corner, around a man with a dolly carting beer into a deli.

At the car, I am shaking so badly it takes several tries to get the key into the lock and again into the ignition and then I am driving.

I follow the river and an old wall and then the street curves around, so that I'm heading uptown. The 59th Street bridge by Trey's apartment is in front of me again.

Africa is in the middle of an Intertropical Convergence where two separate winds meet, one heading north, the other south—like two breaths, two soulful breaths.

The bridge calms me. I find a parking spot a little up from a door-man building. The sun is setting now so that the streets are no longer glowing yellow but look shadowy and blue. I'm still shaking, but I decide to be as objective as possible.

I look up to the sixth floor where Trey lives, where Michael and the Ava Gardner chick are all drunk, where they sit in the dark listening to pigeons and other people's music, smelling their dead rat.

I know that my mother ran away from Forester and Sam and my father. I know how to run. I ran here. I can always run away. But I have no idea how to buzz Trey's doorbell and go in and see who it is that I thought I loved. Love, a subject for young girls, something you get over after you find out what men are really like, after you find out you are not who you thought you were, which is the real problem, everyone walking around not knowing who they are and so attracting some other being to themselves who has nothing to do with who they really are. One thing I know about myself is that I don't usually fight for what I want. It's too embarrassing to lose. It's too humiliating to *want* something. I prefer to admit no need.

I think this as I open the door of my car, step onto the cracked sidewalk, and walk to the door of Trey's building. I wonder if Michael and the chick are even still there. A drop of water falls from the ceiling onto my head. I wipe it away. I ring the buzzer. No reply. I ring the buzzer again. No reply.

I am besieged with panic. Where are they? I must see him. I have not been gone more than fifteen minutes. Fear travels up my spine, grasps my throat. I ring the buzzers. Another and another. I ring every buzzer in the building.

"Who is it?"

"What?"

Buzzzzz.

Someone lets me in. I run up the six flights and to the end of the hall. Trey's door is closed, but unlocked. I turn the knob and walk in and there is no one in the apartment. I stand for a few minutes in the kitchen. The paint is peeling off the floor. I walk back into the hallway. I take the stairs up one more flight and find the door to the roof ajar. I hear a woman's laughter.

I step out onto the tar roof, into a wave of heat.

The bridge is in the background, and Trey is still holding his bottle of J.D., squeezed under his arm as he tries to light a cigarette. Allison sits on the edge, her legs crossed, white and glowing in the dusk. She is half laughing about something. Michael is digging into a pack of cigarettes and reaching his hand out for Trey's lighter. Michael's chick who I call Ava is leaning into him, like they are stuck together at the hip. She is holding a plastic cup.

They all look at me.

"Hi," I say.

"Hi," Trey says, smiling.

I walk over.

"Hey," Allison says.

I don't look at Michael; I'm too afraid.

Trey is easy to look at though; looking at him steadies me, and as I stand there he holds out his bottle of J.D.

I start swallowing. A fire falls down my throat and into my stomach. Rows of lights on the bridge suddenly illuminate.

"Look at that," I say to Trey.

"What?"

"The lights on the bridge."

"Ummmm. They do that every night."

"It's cool."

"Yeah."

Michael clears his throat. I can't look at him, and I have no idea what I should do. I'm still holding the bottle, which has only about two inches of liquor left, so I polish it off.

"Whew," Trey says, as I hand it back.

I go over and sit down next to Allison. I wish it were just a little darker.

Trey hands me a lighted, half-smoked cigarette.

"Still parked in the same spot?" he asks.

"No, I moved," I say. "I'm right over there." I point over the roof.

He nods and sits down next to me.

"Lucky. You've got a lucky streak going for you. I never find a damn parking place."

"You don't have a car," Allison tells him.

"When I rent one," Trey says. "I rent cars all the time."

"We need some chairs," Ava says.

"Chairs," Trey repeats. "I'll tell you what we need," he holds up the empty bottle, "some more whiskey."

"Dope," Allison says.

"Chairs, dope, whiskey," Michael says.

He is still in a suit. I try to think of what day it is. They are so dressed up.

"Michael," I say, my voice cracking, "you're wearing a suit." I know I'm saying the obvious but I can't stop myself.

"Oh yeah," he shrugs, and looks down as though he didn't know what he was wearing.

"Baby, who is this girl?" Ava interrupts. "We haven't been introduced." She comes over to me and holds out her hand. She wears shiny rings and has shiny painted nails.

"I'm Paige," she says, her eyes dark and playful. Her voice is a soprano, strong and almost singing as she talks. She smells faintly of Ralph Lauren perfume. I might like her, if I liked that type at all, except that I'm not in the mood to like anyone right now.

"Paige?" I say, thinking at least it's a nerdy name. At least she doesn't have everything. Her name is not as good as "Ava."

"Michael and I have known each other since high school," she says.

"Oh." I'm surprised again.

"As far as I know he always wears suits. He's a lawyer."

I can't stop myself from laughing. I laugh for a while.

I can't decide if she's a complete fool or if I am.

"Well," I look at him, "what kind of law do you do?"

I speak loudly, but he has stepped away from us and I don't know if he can hear me.

"Honey?" Paige turns around to look at him and then turns back to me. "He does corporate law."

I want to laugh even harder but it occurs to me that this might not be Michael at all, but someone who just looks like him, and it's all a big mistake. I want to stand up and just leave, since it's all a mistake, but I'm feeling dizzy.

"You've known him since high school?" I ask.

"Yeah," she says. "We really do need some chairs, my dress is too nice to sit on the roof with."

"Okay," Trey says, and gets up and disappears into the lighted doorway in the center of the roof.

"Hey, I'll go with you," Michael yells, and lopes across the roof and disappears.

"Yeah, Michael was my high school sweetheart," Paige continues, "we're going to get married."

"Oh," I say again. The liquor suddenly hits me, and I can feel the spin of the earth. "When?"

"Well, we haven't set a date, but we just always knew we would get married."

"Trey's not the marrying kind," Allison pipes up, kindly, I think.

"He's not?" Paige asks, sipping her drink.

"Do you think? No. He's too mistrusting," Allison says.

I feel like I'm going to be sick so I crawl over to the edge of the roof, which is at a slight slant upward, and I lie there looking down at the rows of cars streaming up the street. All their headlights are coming toward me. The tar roof is hot against my cheek. The soprano voice and Allison are still talking, casually, and the horns are honking and there is a slight wind blowing. My head is pounding with sounds, with pain and fire. I grip the edge of the roof and let my head hang down a little, looking at the lights floating up the bridge and the darkness around each light. It looks like the sky on a starry night as you speed though it, falling, like when I used to swing as a kid. When the swing came down out of the sky it fell into a hole in the earth, into my grave.

I hear footsteps, loud behind me, and his voice, the voice I know, not the modified one of Trey.

"What are you doing?"

"Looking at the lights."

He lies down beside me, looking up rather than down, lying on his back.

"They make me dizzy," he says.

"Me too."

"How did you get to be a lawyer?" I ask him.

"I'm not."

"Paige tells me you are."

"I dropped out. I hated it. They teach you how to manipulate a lie into the truth. You would have loved it."

I ignore his last line. "Are you going to marry her?"

"I wanted to. When she was sixteen. I asked her then."

"Why didn't you tell me?"

"Tell you what?"

"That you were going to marry her. That you were a lawyer."

"Because I wasn't going to marry her. And I'm not a lawyer. When you disappeared, I decided what the hell. I told my supervisor I needed to help out my brother; I drove nonstop to New York, hung out with Trey for a day, got drunk and called this girl I used to be in love with. Paige just assumed I had finished law school and was working in New York, and for some reason I never got around to correcting her."

"Like with my mother thing," I say.

Michael makes a sound like he's irritated.

"So what about that suit?" I ask him, "Since when did you own a suit?"

"What's wrong with the suit? This suit is not as weird as your hair."

"Oh, yeah," I say, "I don't know quite how that happened."

"Well, I almost didn't recognize you."

"So, when was the last time you saw her?"

"Who? Oh Paige. When she was sixteen. But Elena," he says.

"Sixteen?" I whisper.

Just then Paige walks up to us.

"We're going inside. It's raining."

"It's not raining," Michael tells her. "Besides, I can't move."

Trey and Allison walk up and stand beside Paige.

"It's raining."

I can see the rain against the headlights so far below.

"Besides, I need that beer we talked about," Paige says.

"Did we talk about beer?" Michael asks.

I sit up. Trey is standing with one arm around Allison and one around Paige.

"We're all going to get beer. Who's going with us?"

"Not me," Michael says.

"I'm watching my car," I say, though I can't exactly see it from this angle.

"Am I the only one around here who can hold my liquor?" Trey asks. "Everyone into the apartment now. It's raining."

And it is, faintly cold and dark wet. I can't see the rain, but it feels like little knives all over my head and back.

"If the liquor store next to the deli is open, we'll be right back, otherwise we'll take a cab around the corner—be back in fifteen or twenty," Trey says.

I can tell Paige is hesitant to go but Trey leads her away, all of them walking across the roof toward the lighted door.

"It's always raining," Michael says, still lying on his back. "Even where we live, in the desert. Have you noticed that? Imagine how rainy Portland must be."

I don't mean to but I swing my head around as I turn back to the headlights moving below us and since he is on his back and I'm on my stomach I hit him in the face with what's left of my hair, and he grabs it and pulls my face to his and kisses me, sloppy and hard, tasting of liquor and salt, but we are together again, as though nothing ever changed, and we manage to get up somehow, from that side of the roof, and walk around to the other side, beyond the door that leads downstairs, to a crevice of mesh fence on the other side of the building, next to a black exhaust pipe pumping out hot air. Michael, with his suit and vodka smell and heavy words, seems like someone else, and I place my hand under his jacket and shirt so I can feel the shape of his body. The rain is cold on my back and his shirt is already soaked. I follow his collar bones with my fingers as they make a v at his throat, which becomes a line down to his sternum to where his ribs veer out to form another, upside-down v, the lines lasting until I reach his hip bones flying off his body, and then another v, from his hips to his groin. I ignore his hard-on and go back up. There is a diamond shape in the center of his body.

In Africa two drops of rain could fill my palm, the drops large diamonds, and within each drop, a yellow fire: the warmth of the sun.

He has me up against the fence, which is cutting my back. My dress is wet and wrapped around my waist, my underwear thrown over the fence behind me, down into the space between the two buildings.

He has my leg up, jammed into the corner of the wall and fence, and I am happy to see him, happy to be with him, had missed him and his body, and even though he smells faintly like Paige, I forget about her in the brutal rain, where there is no yellow fire but only black air and cold wet skin. We are jangling the fence which is between me and a six-floor drop-off into the narrow space between the buildings. We are on the edge of the world, and there is nothing but us. I am crumpling into him and then it all disappears and there is nothing. No breathing, nothing.

Forester gave Elena a ring. A square diamond with translucent blue stones in an antique setting. When she showed it to me she had tears in her eyes.

"It's the most beautiful thing I have ever seen," she whispered, "besides the elephants."

I hear the camera's shutter, my own footsteps, and then a wild string of foreign voices closes in as Elena turns, waving her arm at me while still shooting her camera. Her face registers surprise and then anguish, as she motions me to run.

I do not run; I stand there, her white shirt becoming a waving flag of red and her face distorting as she curls over, sideways, not holding out her hands, falling face-first into the ground.

Later I'm watching from the tree above and they drag her away, her hand with the diamond shooting off sparkles of light falling like glass on my eyes. Everything streams before me; I'm in a forest of water, animal laughter circling.

Michael pushes me further than usual, the fence cutting my back so that I have to let go of my body. It does not always happen, that we hit the same rhythm, so that my body becomes rubber, indestructible, twisting into his body then floating out into darkness and floating back.

My legs tremble and I sit down, crumpling against him, both of us breathing into each other. He holds me tight, my back against his chest.

"You know, Elena," he whispers, "I'm lying to her. Not to you."

I'm in love with him one minute and the next I'm shaking with cold, laughing at something I don't trust.

"That's just the same," I say.

"No," he nods, "it's not the same. It's not the same, Elena."

I glance quickly at him in the dark and think about how, no matter what the context, if you are willing to be fake, you are by nature willing to deceive. And a deceiver will deceive anyone—themselves, someone they don't care about, but especially their friends.

I wonder if this is how he felt when he found out my mother is alive. I feel like that was a simple misunderstanding. This seems more about deceit, about not knowing who you are.

I want to be away from him for a minute. I break away from his arms and stand up.

I fix my clothes and start to walk around the corner toward the lighted door.

"Hey," Michael follows me, pulling my hair a little. "I never lied to you."

"Okay," I say, "and I didn't mean to lie to you."

I continue down the steps to the long tin-tiled peach hallway.

The apartment is dark, but the lights from the other buildings and the bridge shine into the front room, and the light from the hallway shines into the kitchen. Right behind Michael I hear Trey and Allison and Paige clopping down the hallway. They pile into the apartment, onto the futon in the kitchen.

"Baby, how did you get so wet? Your suit!" Paige says to Michael.

Trey looks me over. I'm shaking with cold and dripping water all over his floor.

The three of them just look damp.

"Wow," Trey says, smiling.

"So let me see one of your paintings," I say.

He gives me a look.

"Why don't I show everyone some of my dry clothes?" he says, and goes to his dresser and pulls out some clothes.

Allison lights candles and closes the door and Michael and I slip off our wet clothes and put on jeans and corduroys and t-shirts in the semi-darkness.

"There's the liquor," Trey says, pointing to the futon in the kitchen. He takes a new bottle of J.D. and opens the window over the fire escape and climbs out to have a smoke. Allison follows him, and I find myself in the room with Michael and Paige and she is holding his hand, leaning up against him like a sticker or wet leaf or something and he's not doing anything about it and not speaking.

I love the baggy jeans I'm wearing, the way they slip over my hips when I walk, and the soft and engulfing feeling of Trey's t-shirt.

I decide to follow Trey and Allison out for a smoke. I climb through the window and walk to the end of the fire escape, right next to the stairs. The metal is cold and rusted. Four lanes of headlights pass below us. I'm under an awning so the rain falls beside me. I hold out my hand and let it fill up my palm.

"Did you know about Paige?" Allison asks me.

"No," I say, shaking out my hand.

"That was scummy," she says.

"No," Trey interrupts, "Michael didn't know about Paige. They haven't spoken in years."

"How do you know?" Allison asks.

"'Cause I know. For a couple of years he was depressed about it. They lost track of each other."

"Oh."

Michael and Paige climb out onto the fire escape. She is still stuck to him, but he is looking at me. All five of us line up in a narrow row; Trey and Allison are hunched against the wall, Michael and Paige are leaning against the other apartment's window, and I'm at the top of the stairs.

"So," Paige asks me, "if you're from Albuquerque, how do you happen to be in New York?"

Her voice makes me shudder. In her casual question there is a larger, desperate question.

The rain pours down a gutter behind me.

A month after we had moved to Kenya, Sam, still Elena's husband, showed up in a beat-up blue Peugeot.

He arrived around noon, went for a walk with Elena, and stayed for lunch. Later, as he stood beneath the window of the library, I walked up and joined him. He was in a strange state, tense, and not talking to me. He was listening to the sounds from the library. Elena was moaning in a deep and repetitive voice I had never heard before. Mystified, I walked into the library and saw her lying naked with Forester.

There was for me after that the inability to untangle who belonged to who and who loved who. There had been a string between my mother and father tying them together until Sam knotted it, wrapped himself in it—so that a friend of my father's was now his competition, his enemy. Forester, rich and exotic, untied it all—loosened all strings so that Elena was woven to him by invisible and untouchable means—her emotions unfathomable.

I never understood her choosing someone before she was absolutely certain; this made me afraid, confused, as though all men were interchangeable.

And I know all of this now in the rain, which only heightens Paige's voice, and in her voice I hear that she is quickly trying to tie back the string which connected her to Michael, their past unknown to me, while I see myself free-floating out, above the street, glittering there in sudden uncertainty, knowing I can float endlessly, can fly, knowing also that I can plummet in one unguarded moment. I am uncertain, thinking: musical chairs, random couplings, the music has stopped. Sam must have felt uncertain too, listening to the sound of Elena with Forester, the ground sinking beneath him.

"Say it again?" I ask Paige.

"I asked," she repeats, "if you're from Albuquerque, how do you happen to be in New York?"

"Oh," I speak easily, gathering together my own strings as quickly as I let them loose. "I'm on my way to Africa. My mother died there. Her lover buried her a hundred feet from his window. Now he's selling his land, so I have to go move her body. I have to bring it back." I feel relieved that she is dead again where she belongs and only slightly pained at the idea that Michael will be angry or annoyed.

"Where in Africa?" Trey asks.

"You flying?" Allison interrupts.

"Kenya. Yeah."

"Remind me to give you the *Voice*," Allison says. "Cheap tickets. Or do you already have your ticket?"

"No," I say. "Thanks."

"When did she die?" Allison asks.

"When I was nine."

Trey lights another cigarette. "Ours," he says, "when I was fourteen—Michael, you were sixteen, I guess? The last thing I said to her, I was talking to her on the phone, the connection wasn't that good, and I told her something stupid, like, Michael's smoking like a fiend and we're having a wild party. She laughed. The next morning they got caught in the storm."

His voice is low and I can tell their parents' deaths left them both with a feeling of profound loss, and I admit I don't completely understand that feeling, because to me, Elena's death is more about my freedom.

The rain smell mixes with the car exhaust and I breathe deeply, feeling alive for the first time in a while, happy that my identity is reestablished.

Michael makes a small sound in his throat.

"Where are you going to take her body?" Allison the pragmatist asks me.

"I always imagined it," Trey continues like Allison hadn't spoken, "like just a gray void. They crashed into disorienting gray, disappeared like rain, until Michael told me it was probably beautiful, Macaw feathers flying everywhere, green, blue, red."

I look at Allison.

"Albuquerque," I say, about Elena's body. "Can I bum another?"

Allison lights a cigarette for me, cupping it in the windowsill behind her, then hands it over.

Michael is no longer looking at me.

"You know, Madonna's mom, she died," Allison says.

"Yeah."

"Seems like it made her ambitious," Allison continues.

"It doesn't," Trey interrupts. "It's something else. It makes you not care."

Breaking a still moment, Paige sings out in her soprano voice, "Look, I'm hungry. I have a credit card. Let's order out for Indian food, or Mexican or Chinese or something."

"Okay," Allison says.

"I think," Michael says, "it makes you care more."

And then he turns to Paige and kisses her, in front of us all, a long kiss that seems to last forever and that makes me want to throw myself down the fire escape stairs.

I have no idea what the kiss means, but I sense it's partially in response to my mother story. It might be partially something else too, either some kind of lifelong commitment to her or a long good-bye. I don't know and it feels too weird to wait around to find out.

I stand up and squeeze in between Allison and the window frame and into the apartment. Before too long Allison and Trey come inside too. I go into a dark corner and change back into my still-wet dress.

"I have to go," I tell them.

"Where?"

"The airport."

"You poor thing, you need the *Voice*," Allison says, "but who knows where it is in this mess?"

At dinner, which was often fried frog legs with sliced cucumbers and tomatoes, Sam would quiz me on my multiplication tables and talk about viruses. He would describe in detail how the victims of small-pox looked, or felt, or what the complicated virus did in the body: how it moved about, formed pockets like fingers, and spread billions of its cells about before the body even knew what hit it. It was a subject matter that made me physically reel with discomfort. I remember once, I stared intently at one large yellow-footed lizard as it crawled around on the ceiling with sticky feet and established itself just above Sam. I could see its sides float in and out, and when I concentrated , between the clicks of Elena's nails against her glass, I thought I could hear the lizard breathing. He was preparing for flight, contemplating Sam's head, Sam's plate, the length from the ceiling to the table.

"The world population is almost four billion," Sam said one night, "You can do the math on the back of a matchbook. It took *more than a million years* for the human population to reach one billion. That was in 1800. In 1930, 130 years later, the world population was two billion. In 1960, the world population was three billion. Now, 1975—four billion."

Sam made a look of desolation, like this was a personal problem of his.

"So, what do you think?" he asked me, throwing down his napkin. "Eradicate smallpox or not?"

Sometimes after talking to him I could feel the cells in my body organizing themselves against an imaginary virus. I would imagine them filling with love or fear or anger, or like just now, it is my cells that are re-playing the past, connecting the dots between past and present.

Even inside the apartment I can hear the swish and pull of the cars through the rain, the wet streets echoing the sound.

I thought for a while that I could manage to be immune to everything. I suppose some people are. Not that they couldn't be injected with polio or AIDS or something and not get it, but that they wouldn't care if they did.

Before I was immune to everything, I was terrified of smallpox and polio and all sorts of other things they have immunizations for.

Germ warfare in America years ago involved giving blankets used by smallpox victims to the Indians. The Indians would use the blankets, get smallpox, and entire tribes would be wiped out.

To inoculate is to administer a small amount of the offending virus or bacteria (usually weakened or killed) which triggers the immune system to make antibodies effective enough to ward off the more potent version of that same disease.

The first known deliberate inoculation against smallpox was in 1798, by Edward Jenner, who took the scabs from someone just getting over the illness, ground them up, and rubbed them into an incision in someone well. Then, in 1960, Albert Sabin developed the oral smallpox vaccine.

It was to continue this research on vaccinations and public health that Sam took us to Bamako, Mali. In the Bamako airport, as soon as we arrived, I trailed behind Sam and Elena, listening to Elena's laughter as they walked hand in hand through a moving sea of dark faces. It seemed that everyone roaming the airport had their eyes turned toward me, their vision piercing my lack of color. I became a cloud, ashamed to be looked at, ashamed to be white.

And in the dark of Trey's apartment, with all eyes on me, Michael and Paige together against the window, Allison with a candle walking around making everything bright, I feel the same shame, I inhabit the same insubstantial body and face.

Sam took over a Peace Corps clinic in downtown Bamako. In the center of the examination room stood a shiny aluminum table. To the side of that was a green cabinet filled with little glass jars of vaccinations.

In my dreams I would lock myself in the clinic and take each glass jar of vaccination out of the cabinet. Then I would take a needle, fill it up like I had seen Sam do a hundred times, and shoot myself full of them, vaccination after vaccination.

Along with our frog legs we would take quinine tablets for malaria and salt tablets for dehydration. After a while Sam became more interested in malaria than smallpox.

Smallpox is caused by a virus, whereas malaria is caused by a single-cell parasite that lives in the mosquito. Malaria is the cause of sickle-cell disease, which is an amazing adaptive aberration that renders the person resistant to the most common strain of malaria. It's a genetic alteration of red blood cells that works very effectively until two people with sickle cells have children: for the children inherit red blood cells that are so altered they can be lethal.

They are working on a vaccination for malaria. And although vaccinations are one of the most amazing benefits of modern medicine, many people are questioning multiple vaccinations. Encouraged by the success of eradicating smallpox, the World Health Organization helped to develop vaccinations against several other serious and not-so-serious diseases. But the immune system is a black box, such that if you put a combination of things into the box, the result is not predictable, it varies, and some researchers now think that too many vaccinations are entering the immune system in ways that confuse it, so that it either turns on itself, as with cancer, or simply breaks down, with diseases like asthma, allergies, diabetes, and schizophrenia.

There is always the possibility that any given vaccine can have an undesired effect. Just like any given experience—for example, measles shots have caused heart complications or allergic reactions, and so also, in meeting Michael, I lost my feeling of immunity in trying to live a real life, so that my memory and imagination and reality have all become confused, as though my mind is turning against itself, which is perhaps an adaptive strategy, not unlike sickle-cell disease. My mind and emotions are tricked into a steady-state so that after a while I'm not sure what is real about myself and what is not—a kind of self-mis-recognition, which is what cancer is on an immunological level.

I might be managing to sickle-cell my way into immunity against rejection, but too much immunity and other things surface, like side effects of blocking out pain—neurosis, narcissism, an endless adolescence. The heart is a black box too.

In the narrow room that smells like a dead rat, I am standing underneath a loft bed. It is almost completely dark. Trey is in front of me, and I can tell that for how much he has supposedly had to drink he is not that drunk. He is doing pull-ups off the side of the loft.

I'm shaking, cold again in my thin summer dress, and without underwear.

I want to tell Trey about my mind cross-pollinating cancer and love, immunizations and immunity to love. I know that Michael doesn't much enjoy cross-pollinizations. He thinks them suspect and irrational. And in fact I've noticed that most people who do it are in politics, connecting things that shouldn't rationally be connected.

But Trey is the type to allow things to crisscross into one another, so that in trying to solve one problem, he would know he has to solve all sorts of others as well.

I can tell this about Trey, as he tells me to undress and put back on his clothes. As he tells me that Michael has lost his mind and that he'll get it back. As he does his pull-ups, wide-gripped, fast.

"A long time ago," I tell him, while I put his jeans on in the darkness, "I used to think love was like it is in the songs. You know: baby you're so beautiful, baby come closer; baby our love's so wild it's gonna take me away; baby I love you but we're better off alone; we're going down now baby, get away. And with the drums and guitars and the voice of some guy or some girl, raging and about to break down, it could set me on edge. It could make me think I might know about love. It could almost make me think I might be in love, even if the one I loved was absent."

"Or nonexistent," he says.

"Yeah. Or that," I say.

"You warmer?" he asks.

"Yeah."

"Well, if you weren't here for Michael, I might play you a song," he says.

"Maybe I'm not here for him after all," I say.

"You are. Don't forget that. You are. And I won't forget it either," he says. "I don't believe in tampering with that kind of thing."

That's what the complexity problem is about, I want to tell him. It's too late not to tamper with things.

Allison walks in the room with a candle, illuminating Trey's face.

"Take the Concord," she says to me. "It's faster than the speed of sound. Goes right into Paris. I took it once."

"Sounds expensive," I tell her.

"Um," she says, "it was a while back. My dad paid for it so I don't know. You sure you don't want to leave in the morning instead? After some coffee?"

"No, I'm ready to go."

"It's still raining," Trey says.

"It doesn't matter."

I can feel a silence gathering around me.

I say that my mother died in Africa in 1975 because you can watch someone who is dead walk and laugh and put on lipstick and dress and undress for someone, for the shower, for sleep, and still they are dead. We all know this already. Though after she died I could no longer hear her breathe. No matter how close I stood next to her— even if she was playing tennis, there was no sound from her mouth.

In the Land Rover everyone was quiet as the elephants roamed around. I thought everyone saw them breathing in through their trunks, the air swirling through their bodies until they exhaled into the sky where their breath circled the sun and came back.

But the men must not have seen, because their guns snorted out short and rapid exhalations, not ever taking in the world, only blindly giving.

After they shot the elephants I didn't hear any breathing. I watched Elena's neck to see the pulse. I listened to the wind. There was nothing. Only calm, like before something happens. Like before you shoot. That calm lasted for years.

And then I met Michael.

I spent a lot of time listening to Michael breathe. I spent a lot of time seeing Michael's breath circle around the sun and come back.

But here is the calm again. The whole apartment is quiet, even with the disco music playing a few floors below and the rain making the traffic echo up louder.

"Good-bye," I say to everyone, and walk out.

Michael is in the hallway, drunk, telling me I'm too drunk to drive.

"I'm not," I shrug.

He is in the stairway, telling me it's raining too hard to drive.

But I walk downstairs, absorbed with only the silence, the wonder of that silence. How strange that it should hit me now.

I do find Kennedy airport, about four hours later, after several wrong turns and a few stops at seedy-looking gas stations. At the airport I discover all the ways to get to Nairobi. Through Paris. Through London. Through Zurich. Spur-of-the-moment cheap flights are not so easy to find, and many of the airline counters are closed. I pick one with a chipper uniformed woman. It is two in the morning. Her flights go through Zurich. My first credit card is rejected, and then my second card is rejected. It doesn't seem possible. I remain standing but I feel like collapsing; I can't hear what the lady is saying. All of my effort is in vain.

"Give me your phone number," I tell the lady. "Your direct line."

The airline woman is no longer chipper. Her mouth is a tight, pursed o. She hands me a piece of paper with a number on it.

I walk over to a pay phone. I punch in my phone card number. My mother answers on the third ring.

I tell her where I am and that she has to call the airline and give them her credit card number and that I'll pay her back.

"Going to Africa is not a good idea," she tells me.

"Why not?"

"Too expensive, for one thing," she says.

"I'll pay you back," I say.

"It's silly and impulsive and immature," she spits. "I expected more of you. This is ridiculous. You should turn around and drive home immediately. Plus it's the middle of the night here, I can't think."

"It's the middle of the night here too, and this is an emergency. I have to go," I tell her, "and I'll pay you back."

"You don't have the money to pay me back," she says.

"Please," I say. "It's important."

"Okay," she says. Her fight is gone. She'll call and pay for the ticket.

I ask her about the elephants and her diamond ring. I ask her about Forester and Africa.

"Blotto," she says. "I remember blotto. I was completely blotto."

She talks like she's holding in her breath. Like she's holding in a hit.

I want to say to her, exhale. Exhale. You can only hold your breath so long.

A breath can take you up to God. A breath can take you down to Hell.

Inhale. Exhale. Inhale. Exhale.

5

I am stuck in a booth with some kind of supervisor at 6:00 A.M. dealing with my lack of a visa. Even though he is on the opposite side of a wide metal desk, I can smell him. It's sweat or hair oil or bad breath or some of all of that. I have a plane ticket, which he is flicking in his hands, but besides the visa, I also lack the recommended vaccinations, which he is making some spurious issue of. He is a serious man, and every five minutes or so he puts my ticket down and takes a handkerchief out of his pocket, folding it over both his fat pinkies, and stuffs the cloth halfway up both his nostrils. Any subject matter takes on a long pause until this activity is over. The first time I ignored it, now it is so disgusting that I'm pressed to the wall in revulsion.

After two phone calls interrupt us, he slicks his hair back and hands me back my ticket. "You'll have to buy your visa upon entering the country. Bad idea."

He gives me a stern look but I stare into his eyes until he stands up and leads me out.

I spend an hour in the airport bathroom, changing into black pants and a white shirt and fooling with my hair. I'm glad it's chopped off. I feel unrecognizable, like the supervisor never actually saw me—I'm in disguise. I should have gone undercover long ago. I should have dyed my hair black and added spikes, like the girl I met.

It doesn't really occur to me until we are in the air and over the ocean that there is no way I can get off the plane. This is obvious, but the severity of this condition seizes me and I break into a cold sweat. I want to get off the plane. I don't actually think I have any business going to Africa.

Once we've landed in Zurich I'm more calm, and from Zurich to Nairobi I spend my time sleeping and watching a fly buzz around the plane. I wonder if it is a Swiss fly or an African fly, and if it'll manage to deplane.

My airplane crowd blends into another crowd and I end up following three military men through the Nairobi airport. They walk only two feet in front of me, muddy rifles slung over their shoulders, splattered the same color as their mud-covered uniforms, their boots tracking the floor. To my amazement, I pass right through the gate where they are checking for visas. There seems to be an entire army in the airport and I'm waved through into a large central room where I am free to leave.

I pass a woman wrapped in a bright yellow cloth selling coconut-flavored coffee, but most everyone else around me is dressed in European-style clothes. I move into the languid heat. I can't get a deep breath.

I haven't read up on Nairobi, and there do not seem to be the buses I was imagining. I feign boredom and ennui and walk over to a taxi sign. I can feel eyes following me.

In the taxi, speeding toward the bus station, the *matatus*, I close my eyes and see our collision, the raging heat, the bloody end.

But we arrive at the bus depot. The sign is bleached out, and a small bus sits crookedly with a flat tire that someone is yelling about. The hot wind carries the iron smell of blood. I feel eyes watching me. I diligently search a map on the wall for the route that will take me to Forester's.

A man hits me softly on the arm with the back of his hand.

"Jambo," he says. He has a wandering eye, or more like a permanently fixed eye, stuck looking in the direction of his nose.

He thrusts a paper bag at me. It is filled with orange gummy candy in the shape of worms.

"Try lady, I know you come with me. I show beautiful parks. I show you. Try you like lady, orange flavor candy. You try."

I'm thinking maybe this is the wrong bus stop. I'm thinking maybe I should call Forester, which I do not want to do. The man in front of me has brown teeth, and his button-down polyester shirt is brown, tucked in tight around his thin belly.

"Unasema KiEngereze?" he asks. He's asking me if I speak English.

Naturally, I don't know a word of English. I make up a few sounds in some combination of Swedish and French. He's not convinced, so I just repeat *no, merci, no, no.*

I need to go south. Forester lives near Tsavo National Park, the east side of it, and only one bus will drop me off on the main road and I don't see it listed on the board. Since I can't suddenly remember my English in front of the man offering me candy, I walk around until I find a tourist brochure with a map, which doesn't look very helpful, and brings him to ask me more questions.

"Where you go? I help you." His breath is hot and sour in my face, and his hands are crinkled with different colors of dirt in the creases. He grabs my brochure, "Where you go? I know where you go."

I turn around and walk away, pissed off that I'll probably miss my bus. He runs after me and drops the paper on the floor at my feet.

There are a few men standing around watching us. I turn and pick up the map. I finally see on the map where the main road is, and I walk up to a driver and point to it. He points me to another bus, no words exchanged. I step up onto the next bus and point to the map. The driver nods. "Yes, I go there," he says in perfect English.

The gummy-worm man stays in the parking lot, his hand in the paper bag.

The *matatus* claims to be air-conditioned but most of the windows are down and the air is thick with cigarette smoke. There are flies buzzing around. I choose a seat next to a woman who doesn't look at me. We sit in the bus for exactly one hour and forty minutes before it leaves. I ask once when it will leave but the driver just shrugs. And then finally we are moving, and fast, as though to make up for lost time. The streets are crowded with cars and the sights are not too unusual—a Barclays Bank and a Mobil gas station, an ad for British Airways and palm trees, so that it all feels like some European city mixed in with Los Angeles, except for a huge carcass of an animal being carried across the street by two men, and except for the way the bus is careening around the cars, like our bus is chasing some large rabbit.

On our way out of town I see aluminum houses propped up with boards, invaded by bushy trees, laundry hanging out across scraps of metal. The landscape is green and dusty at the same time, dust flying in the windows even though we're on a paved road. For a while we are stopped in traffic and some people get off the bus and walk along beside it and yell and get back on. My eyes and throat sting from the smoke. Together all of these smokers must have finished off at least two cartons of cigarettes. The driver stops the bus and helps a man put a goat in the back. After a while there are just four of us on the bus. When we turn off onto an old highway with cracks in the asphalt and no lines down the middle, I recognize the slope of the hills behind the road. There are signs and a new gas station and a flat scrappy carpet of pistachio-green weeds along the highway, and then I see the rust-colored clay road with the wooden sign that says Ecco.

I yell to the driver to stop, and I stagger through to the front of the bus and disembark. I walk back the thirty feet to the barbed-wire fence that is still standing, low and tangled, and follow along the half-mile of Forester's private driveway.

I walk toward a blue-washed sky, a breeze blowing my hair, amazed at it all, until my heart takes over. It beats very fast for several seconds then stops all together, for maybe six or seven beats, and I know, am convinced, that my time is up. I stand still on the road wondering if it will resume, but it beats so fast in high gear that I can tell it's not even pumping blood. It's just beating for itself, so I sit down in the middle of the road. I trace a line in the red dirt with my finger. I think about how I've never been to a cardiologist or seen a cypress tree or traveled to Australia or South America or jumped out of a plane. And how I never said what I wanted to say to Michael—and then my heart is beating again, normally, so I stand up and continue walking.

There is a man in the front yard, looking west. It happens to be Forester himself, the rounded hills falling flat behind him. The way he is standing makes me think about how space is an arc, that straight out in front of me will take me nowhere other than back to where I came from. He is watching a small girl, far off in the yard, as she runs after a pig the same size as her. I walk up the gravel drive and he turns his head slightly. He seems to look right through me, like a wild animal might. I am standing about thirty feet away but I think he hasn't seen me, and I am overwhelmed with the sensation that I should retreat. I think about where I could go. And then something about the way he moves his head, just inches to the right, I know he's watching me. I'm in the roving scope of his rifle eyes, but he's still pretending to be a part of the hills and the poles and the yard, like I'm some stupid animal caught upwind.

"Well, well," he finally says, walking toward me, "Elena."

It might literally be the smoke from his joint, but he has around him a haziness, as though his energy is dispelling the air molecules and making him hard to see. Or maybe it's the sun. I squint at him.

"How did you get here?"

"*Matatus.*"

He raises his eyebrows and smirks, "Lucky then. Would you like a hit of dagga?"

"No thanks," I say, but he hands it over, half a joint. His laugh is friendly, but his look surrounds me like the summer sky. His eyes float over me the same as any man's. And he shifts his weight the same. And he's watching me and waiting for me to take it and I'm feeling lost, already taken in by his world, so I set my duffel bag down and take a deep drag. It feels like a knife cut down my throat. I hate weed. I cough uncontrollably, collect myself, my eyes watering, and inhale again. I look him over. He's wearing snakeskin sandals, a strange blanket around his waist, and a thin unbuttoned camel-colored shirt, the sleeves rolled up. He picks up my bag and begins walking, taking a tattered pack of cigarettes and a lighter out of his shirt pocket with his free hand. He sets down the duffel bag to light two cigarettes.

"Actually, I don't smoke," I say, not wanting to get any closer and still employed with the joint.

"That's too bad. Smoking is one of the great pleasures of life," he says, and hands me the cigarette, which I take with my left hand.

He laughs, "So how old are you now?"

Even a slight movement, his hand to his face, makes muscles ripple and twitch and move in his chest, his arms, his neck. He is thin while still being full up with these muscles. They make me nervous—they are somehow too noticeable.

"And what are you doing here?" he asks. "You could have missed me, you know. I'm due in Japan in a week. Veda wouldn't know you from Adam. The other thing, I was expecting your mother."

I don't intend to answer but it doesn't matter anyway, as he's already walking away with my bag toward his front door, "You wanna do something wild when you're here," he says, walking backwards to talk to me, "get a small *scratch*. I've lived here twenty years, been bit by a puff adder, gored by a rhino, always had some strain of malaria, and this *scratch, not even* a scratch, gave me lymphangitis—the red stripe up your arm—and I had an allergic reaction to the antibiotic they gave me—I had no white blood cells at all, that's what kills you, not a lion or yellow fever—no. A *scratch*. I went to hell and came back. It was fantastic. I recommend it."

He stops at the veranda, puts down my duffel bag, and throws his cigarette to the ground. He introduces me to his wife and child, Veda and Mira. Veda speaks perfect English but with a clipped accent, and she's wearing riding attire, looking like royalty. Mira is around three, with dark curly hair and black eyes, in a shiny red bathing suit. There are other people around, Veda's friends, other children, a few others in white, a cook, a gardener. Forester speaks at length to a couple visiting from Spain. When no one is looking I throw my cigarette and joint to the ground with Forester's. Veda hands me a lemonade and I stroll around on the veranda sipping the tangy drink.

Forester is nice, friendly, funny. But he is a man I would never dare to carve out a space for myself in, even casually, and I am surprised that Elena tried. It is obvious from his short conversations that he is a man who views life and death as one, a man who has no sentimentality, no regrets. Life simply is what it is—in his view: brutal, base, absurd. I wonder if he was the same man when Elena knew him.

The hard edges of his elbows and eyes seem to be all around me. He puts his hand on my shoulder and motions me inside.

"So," he says, "there is a striking resemblance."

He's making fun of me.

"You mean I'm not as beautiful," I say, as I walk through the entryway and stand before the full-length mirror at the end of the hall.

"I didn't say that. In fact, you're a bit of a shock."

This mirror has always been here, gold-gilded and haunted. When I was nine, the mirror was a force field that could pull me in with one glance. I knew what it would do—it would slip my clothes off, dissolve them even, and if I kept walking toward the mirror, it would silently kill me. In my dreams, everyone on earth followed a road around the world that came to an end at the mirror in

Forester's hallway. They take one look in the mirror, stand for a moment in their nakedness, then crumple in death.

Glancing into the mirror now, I see the strange haircut and that same pale, empty look that usually comes out of Elena's eyes, and I cringe. I focus my eyes so that the energy goes outward instead of just staying still, and then I divert my gaze.

This may sound like a lie but it's true: I never think much about my looks. Maybe some days I'm beautiful, or feel beautiful, and some days I'm not, but I don't worry about it. Or at least I never did worry about it, until I stood in front of Forester. And with Forester, not even being especially attracted to him, thinking mostly of him as an old man who has some information I want, I nonetheless become self-conscious. I think I'm probably ugly, and I never even knew before how ugly. I think, no wonder Michael left, no wonder he was with that beautiful girl. And I think back to my beginning with Michael, and how even when I was dying to know what Michael thought of me, I never thought much about my looks. I should have. I should have paid attention to every detail of my appearance. Because suddenly I see that I am horribly flawed.

I assume most people know that beauty is never what it promises to be. The first time I saw Michael he was just an apparition on the mesa; a man who looked as though he had walked around the world: jeans, white shirt, a water walk. When he came closer, with the light shining on him and his smile promising me the world, I should have paid attention. I should have known that nothing would come of it.

I am standing beside Forester as he points to the python skin, six feet long, thousands of triangles brown and darker, one after the other, hanging on the wall beside the mirror. He is saying something extreme about how he killed it, but I am listening to the way his voice has lowered in tone, noticing the way he again has his hand on my shoulder, leading me into the next room, and it is then that I accidentally glance back at the mirror and it happens—I am stripped naked, my skin and my face no longer hiding the fact that I am just a pile of disembodied limbs.

"Recognize anything?" he asks.

I hate that mirror, I almost tell him, but we have already entered another room. I try to recover. There is still the lion skin in the library. I remember various guests being impressed with a few of the paintings. They mean something to me now: a Jasper Johns, a few Warhols and Rothkos, several Picasso pencil and charcoal sketches, a Turner, all mixed in with photographs of every kind. And between these, the walls are covered with tapestries, clay and African beads, masks, animal skins. In the bedroom there is not one inch of wall space left uncovered.

"What animal is that?" I point to a small beautiful skin next to the Rothko.

"A civet cat. One of the few spotted cats left. Quite endangered."

I point to his old turntable, "I remember that. And I remember your old records, and the wooden speakers." I stand next to one. It is covered with plants and fiery glass bongs. "They are still huge, as tall as my hips."

"Pah. I never use them. Too much bass. But half the records— the particular recordings—not even available today. It's a crime. I have to record them myself. Come and listen to the new system— it sounds live."

I follow him back into the living room, where I run my hand along the zebra skin couch that has the matching end table. The house smells of incense. He shows me his new system with the Vandersteen speakers and talks about the sweet spot, which is the best position to be in for the most perfect sound.

In the kitchen, Veda watches as her cook places food on the table. She is relaxed, and smiles as she speaks, but she is exacting in both her speech and manners, and I get the distinct feeling I will be poisoned by the food. She insists I drink Absinthe and eat Orynox and a strange dish of vegetables and fruits broiled with *nazi,* coconut juice. Forester drops his napkin on the floor and uses the same fork for the entire meal, and I tell her I've had a long day and can't eat much. She is plainly insulted, and Forester smirks. The incense and Forester's smoking gives me a headache and I retreat to my guest room. I lean back on the saggy pullout couch and look at the pale rose-colored walls. I close my eyes.

Someone knocks on the door. I sit up. It is bright outside. I open the door. Veda stands there, her hair up and her clothes neat—a dress with a belt.

"How are you feeling?"

I can't bring myself to speak.

"Would you like anything?"

I just stand there.

She smiles, tucking a few stray hairs behind her ears. "It's the next day. One o'clock."

"Oh," I say.

"I have *nazi* hen, creamed vegetables, and papaya ice cream. Come."

I follow her into the dining room, and then realize I must look a mess, sleeping all night and half a day, so I run back and brush my hair and teeth and return to the table.

Veda asks casually what I'm doing here.

"I don't know," I tell her.

This doesn't seem to bother her. "Well," she shrugs, "there is much to do."

"Yeah," I say.

"I can give you some recommendations," she says, slowly bringing the last forkful of creamed vegetables to her mouth.

Forester is not finished with lunch, his plate sits half-full, but he's been wandering around the house, through the living room, padding around barefoot, and he drops a stack of magazines on the table beside me, next to my plate. He takes away a few and drops others. He disappears and reappears with more magazines, shaking them out, flipping through one or two. His sleeve brushes against my bare arm, and I smell his soap and smoke and the magazine dust.

"Tonight," Veda says to Forester, "I must take Mira and go to Nairobi, to see my mother. We planned it a week ago, to stay there the night."

"Fine," Forester answers her.

She turns to me. "You will be here when I get back?"

"I assume so," I say. "Thanks for lunch."

"You are finished?"

"Yeah, we're finished," Forester interrupts. "It was great, Veda," he says, barely looking at her.

He points to the stack. "Check out these magazines. In some of them you'll find Elena's photos."

Veda's composure flickers as she stands and snaps her fingers for the cook to take away the plates. Forester turns up the music, blasting Schubert all over Kenya.

"The baby's ears," Veda yells. But she doesn't act to change anything, and Mira is already outside playing on the veranda.

The magazines he slams down all around me are from the 1960s and '70s, stacks totaling at least fifty in front of me. He keeps taking them from a closet in the entry hall. *Life, Time, National Geographic, Paris-Match,* German *GEO,* British *Vogue, Rolling Stone,* an occasional *Playboy.* He flips through them with some care, but in haste, looking, dropping them to the floor, bringing out more.

Finally a German *GEO.* He flips through it, throws it open.

The photos in the *GEO* have little captions that say FOTO, *Elena Monroe.* There is one photo I remember her taking, a woman on the Niger River with a neck almost the size of a basketball. In *Life,* photos from the Ivory Coast, guards with machine guns pointing at the camera. And elephants, tusks cut off, lying in blood, a baby elephant standing nearby, all too heavy to look at, too painful to look at twice.

Forester slaps down beside me a manila folder, aged and yellow, filled with a whole series of gruesome prints of bloody elephants with the sides of their faces cut off.

"Poachers," Forester says. "There should be a couple in there where they killed a baby for a tusk the size of your thumb. And some of those—mixed in with her other 5:00 A.M. excursions, are the last photos she took. She became a good tracker. Had a knack for it."

"She took these?"

"Yeah."

"Did you ever go with her?" I ask, looking through the photos.

"Of course. I got her started. I took her on the first one, and several after. But the elephants broke her heart. I had a friend over here once—he was a friend of Truman Capote's who wanted to buy a huge ivory penis for him. Capote had a thing for ivory. Anyway, for some reason Elena fixated on the elephants, as if they're the only species in trouble. She had too much to drink one night, as usual, and screamed at Casey—that was Capote's friend—screamed until she was blue—created a real scene. I loved that about her. She wasn't afraid to say anything, regardless of who she was talking to. She wasn't too bright in that way. You want to succeed, you have to remember the world is a woman—seduce, then conquer, and don't get emotionally involved. She started in on the elephants, claimed they had extra intelligence."

"They *are* supposedly—"

"They're also fun to shoot." Forester inhales deep on his cigarette and throws the burning butt into the kitchen sink. "And a Hong Kong ivory mover used to make a million a week. So there you go. Hey, let me see your hand." He tucks a few magazines under his arm and takes my right hand in his. He is looking at the visible raised scar marks across my knuckles. He has blue-gray eyes, I notice, and tanned, manicured hands.

"Wow, you still have the scars," he says, his cigarette breath in my face.

"What are they from?" I ask him.

"Not sure. Some kind of snake, poisonous frog, insect. You don't remember?"

"No."

"Well, that's understandable. You didn't remember then either. Must have been painful, though. Your whole arm was swollen up twice its size."

I notice I'm shaking. I notice that I have not stopped shaking since I got here. It is a kind of trembling, invisible and internal, until just now. Now my hands are not steady, each photograph I hold jitters in the air for several seconds until I put it down.

"I see images, sometimes," I blurt out.

"What kind of images?"

"I guess from that day, you know. Other days too. The elephants."

"Yeah, don't we all," he says.

I help him carry some of the magazines back to the closet.

And there, hanging above the stacks of magazines, a gold dress Elena used to wear, and the white Dior with the slit up the side, and several others.

"I can't believe this. They're still here," I say, gliding my hand down the gold dress, a sequined, elastic material that crackles a little as I touch it.

"Oh yeah, she left with nothing."

"Nothing?"

"Nope. Not even you. Remember? You flew back alone. A couple of weeks later."

"I don't remember."

"No? She never talks about it?"

"No."

"Well," he says, "take the shit if you want it."

"I like the gold dress."

"Take it."

It crinkles into my arms as I carry it back to my room. It still smells faintly of Chanel No. 5. The threads are old, and splay out gold dust when pulled, shedding a drunken light. I slip on the dress, and the clingy soft and silky gold threads seem to manifest the same sadness as my mother. It shimmers, diamond-like, when I move. I slip into my black heeled sandals and put on lipstick, and pull my hair up like she used to, a twisted, half-falling bun.

I don't look like her when I look in the mirror, but I don't look like myself either, if I ever did—it is an altogether new creature. I walk out into the living room.

Forester is sitting on the zebra skin couch taking the seeds out of some buds.

I walk around and look at the pictures on his walls.

"Baby," he says, "you make me long for those parties again. I think her suitcase is in there somewhere. That would have more of her things."

I walk over to the wall and open a door. It's not the same closet.

"Over there," he points.

I move over a few feet to where he seems to be pointing. The wall is made of long dark boards, from floor to ceiling, like a ship or old-fashioned library.

I run my fingers along the wall.

"Hotter, hotter," he says.

My fingers fall on a small metal handle embedded into the wood. I pull it, nothing happens. I push it, and the door swings open. The Dior dress, the magazines.

"Maybe not that one," he says, "the next one."

I look around for another metal groove. In this closet, four feet over, there are boxes, tools, and books, and in the corner, her suitcase, a round dirty-white American Tourister.

Besides various clothing items and one towel and one sheet, there is a small 3 x 5 notebook, with the gas mileage information for the car she had at the time, and a few French words and phrases translated into English. Most of the objects in the suitcase are as insignificant as the gas mileage notebook. There are two international certificates of vaccination as approved by the World Health Organization claiming that Elena Monroe was revaccinated against smallpox in 1975, and also given a cocktail shot for yellow fever, cholera, typhoid, and hepatitis. Signed by Sam Fraizer, M.D., and stamped in Bamako.

The scent of her dress is beginning to overtake me and I fight an intense wave of fear.

Occasionally, randomly, I have inhaled this same perfume, in the middle of a restaurant, or walking down the street, and the smell always disorients me, so that I will be plunged unexpectedly into danger. I usually try somehow to escape it. But it seems right now that the fear is in everything, and I can't fight it, so I just look through it, at all the objects, like the photos in the suitcase. They are small black-and-white prints: a starving woman made of sticks, crawling toward a dead tree as though she is the missing branches of that tree, fallen and stepped on. A photograph is supposed to be about the subject being photographed, but sometimes, if you know how to look, you can see with the eyes of the person who took it, and with their eyes you feel what they felt.

I show it to Forester.

"Another famine, the usual story," he says, standing beside me now, flicking briefly through the rest.

"That's the most wonderful perfume—" he says.

"It's on her dress."

"Reminds me of her. You know, Elena was ambitious. I never paid attention to that because she was so sexy. You can't take a woman seriously if she's too sexy. All you want to do is screw her."

I step out onto the veranda so I don't have to say anything. The wind blows around me. Forester's music is as loud outside as inside.

There is a dead tree in his yard near the fence, like a massive hand reaching toward the sky.

Looking out I have to admit that I have somehow confused this place with other places. Or more accurately, have confused my memory with my imagination. For example, I knew that just beyond the fence I could see elephants, impalas, and wildebeests on the horizon, and now there is nothing except strange trees in the way. The air is musty, smelling like rust and animals. The wind has not stopped blowing since I arrived, always a breeze wandering over the land, across my face.

It is a land that seems to change as a face changes, so that I recognize the spirit before me but not the place, ravaged and difficult to see.

I've lived most of my life worried about believing in something that isn't true. Thinking someone loves you and finding out they don't—that they never knew you. Or that I believed something about the way the world was and it turned out I was wrong. For example, there is a creator after all, one true God—or believing that —it's all just some lucky chance after all: molecules colliding into place.

Michael used to make me think of God, now he makes me think of chance. How ineffectual and narcissistic it is to conform the world and its origin and purpose to my experience. And I do the same with Africa, or at least the Africa I can see from Forester's porch, which seems to embody both, seems to breathe with a divine spirit and crackle apart into random meaningless parts a moment later.

I walk around the veranda as it follows the house into the back. The long stretch of grass where Forester used to place his Steinway is before me, and a whole line of Acacia trees on the far edge of the yard, beyond the hot tub.

I stand for a long time, the big disc of the sun shimmering, taking up half the sky as it descends into the dark-blue horizon.

The moon will rise up above the Acacia and wild olive trees. I walk down, across the lawn, toward the trees. The ground is uneven and I have to step slowly. I am far away from the house, but I can hear a few men talking, their fragmented Swahili carrying on the wind. And in these voices I hear Forester, and feel a familiar fear and anticipation. In the dusk I can see the outline of the men standing on the veranda.

I stand under the row of trees and look across the yard to Forester's bedroom window. He used to clear the ground out around the trees, for picnics and lounging, so the usual assortment of ants and bugs would be less common. I lie down on the ground to look above me at the dark branches. The ground is warm, the same temperature as my body. A few of the trees at the far end are filled with weaverbird nests, and something is making sounds, either the birds or some kind of cricket or cicada.

The whole place feels like a slowly enveloping drug. I can almost see the luminous linen-covered tables from 1975. I'm not even sure who I am. There is really nothing here that can hold me to my former identity.

Forester's voice has disappeared, but I can smell his burning weed. I sit up. I look around in the dim light, turning in a circle to see if anyone is around, to see where Forester is, the wind shifting, blowing in my face, across my ears, and in circling I see that there is a stone slab breaking out of the ground about twelve feet to my left, a bit behind me. A thin upright slab. A gravestone.

It takes me a long time to walk over to it. One small spot on earth, but I imagine it is infinitely deep.

It is a cold and smooth marble stone, black-blue with the way the end of the sky is shining on it, and I can barely read in the end of the light: Elena Monroe. Dearly Beloved. August 15, 1942 to December 20, 1975.

I immediately believe what I see—I feel the reality of it in my body—and I blame myself, my stupid habit of lying about it has made it come true. My hands shake.

I can sense my logic is off, having spoken to a woman in Albuquerque not long ago who I know to be my mother, and yet here is the proof before me, that all I have said and felt is true. She is dead. Buried here.

I feel like I'm in a slow spin.

I feel the smooth surface of the stone, and the rain-drenched surface of Michael's body, my desire, our sidestep into shadow where the fence hit the insides of my arms. I can feel the diamond shape of his bones, bringing me here to this spot on the earth, my heart skimming across the ground, my path crossing his where my life line hits the heart line, intersecting until we circle like water, the way the waves go out all over.

I will stay here forever, all of it circling until it crumbles around me.

Some of the lights in the house go on, others go off. The veranda and the yard are illuminated in a deep yellow, but the lights by the hot tub are red, and the ones over the back windows are blue.

A few minutes later, music blasts out of the windows, disembodied non-narrative voices call over and around the drums and into the night, and in between the voices, a frantic, desperate shuffling, an unending beat, and I feel it like I might feel the beauty of a machine gun taking me down; the sounds gather in my chest and throat as small clusters of loss.

And then he comes walking up, a dark easy shadow, his shoulders back, his clothes flapping with each step. The gold dress seems to tighten around my chest and my heart has stopped again, so that I'm waiting to see if it will resume.

I'm kneeling on the ground, which I don't know until I open my eyes and see the outline of Forester standing above me, looking down at me, his eyes slits of light.

He hands me a drink, ice-cold, the glass wet.

"This is where the airstrip will go, straight through these trees, straight through the house. Airstrips follow the prevailing wind."

So he knows what I'm here for, I think, to get her body.

I wonder whether or not I spoke to Elena at the airport. Perhaps I didn't. Perhaps my credit card worked and I simply got on the plane.

Forester is shuffling his feet on the ground, and I'm gauging the distance from his bedroom window to her gravestone to see if it's really one hundred feet. It's closer to two hundred. Forester looks me over and clears his throat. He feels like an animal stalking me, though he is just standing there. He feels like a man who could make me forget everything.

I taste my drink. Rum and Coke, mostly rum.

"I'm going to miss this place," he says, his voice low.

I am trying to calculate when the feral animal next to me is going to attack, and this makes me miss it, the slow and subtle way it comes upon me, so that he doesn't act as much as I do—so that even knowing I'll never get through to him, get through to where he is buried inside that smirk, that cloud of smoke, that sarcasm, I still hear meaning in our conversation when there is none.

"Why is this here?" I ask.

"To help me remember."

"Remember what?"

"That there's no place for innocent optimism. She told me she wanted to be cremated, but—"

"This land must be worth a lot," I say, to put an end to it.

"Maybe," he says slowly, leaning into the wind. "Depends on whether or not you're willing to die for it."

I feel the cool marble stone against my back, and I drink half my drink fast and flick the rest so that the liquid flies out to my left, landing in flat, quick drops. I contemplate asking him if he had loved my mother, or if she loved him, or what was going on back then. But Forester bends down toward me and the sky becomes an enclosure I can't, or don't want to, get out of.

He is warm and tastes like rum. His eyes glint at me in a way that tells me they are my entrance into the abyss. I want to go in. I want to see if there is an end to it. I am beating the earth with my heart pumping out of control; the earth will open up beneath me. We will fall. The music ripples over our bodies and the voice that has spoken for me changes, is always changing, so that in the great tide of life we are each one blade of grass.

I slide my hand along the dirt beneath me and onto his flank, his ribs, his arms sharp-edged. He moves slowly but violently, lifting the dress, pulling it off so that I am a snake shedding its skin, bare-chested below him.

I remember the smooth ice-wind of Michael's voice, *you're my breath.*

Forester is also naked, quickly, his wet tongue all over me, leaving me limp.

"People can forget anything they want," Forester whispers. "I had forgotten."

My body shakes with every word I think to say and can't.

I feel his breath against my chest; I see his face rise in an arc above me, the sky unfurling, the guitars and voices calling me.

His eyes are a vacuum pulling me in. He runs his hand up my inner arm and it is like a knife, a straight cut, from wrist to elbow, deepening near the elbow, the blood immediate, the white tendon pushing out.

The knife of his hand slides across my face, so that my eyes have no skin, my cheekbone juts out, ivory white. Blood streams my face and arms in thin, lazy waves. My arms open, their blood flowing around his neck so that he is covered as I hold tight to him, her spirit around him, so that I know it again. My cheekbones are bare, without flesh. He pounds me, drunk with rum, with music, beating me, spreading my legs wider, taking off my face, taking me toward her.

A body falling over itself, from white to red.

The elephant doesn't have a face. The tusks, the skin all around the tusks, gone.

Elena doesn't have a face, and Sam is ripping his shirt off, yelling, pounding Elena's chest, kissing her, breathing into her. He arches back, his face to the sky, as though pleading, then his eyes open and stay that way and footsteps, a gunshot, shake the air. His eyes tell me nothing they are supposed to, they tell me things I don't want to know. And then I am picked up and thrown, farther away into the green.

There is running and yelling until I am high above them, my feet where their heads had been. I am there so long that green streams before my eyes, a forest of water, light falling like glass on my eyes, animals howling around me.

It is Forester that reminds me. It is the way he enters me like lead, a slow heat that makes me want to crumple over, makes me see the skin pulled back, white cartilage, the vibrations of the earth everywhere, directing me to one small point of time, my ears attuned now, altering the way my feet drag across the earth, so that I finally hear the low voice of the elephants, long sound vibrations that can travel far, bending over and around objects. I hear their screaming over Forester's body, across the yard, even with the music endlessly shuffling in the shifting wind, I know something. The smell of death. Of life. My life. His body.

"God, woman," he breathes, "who are you?"

The stars move on with white velocity.

I almost ask him the same thing.

He is on his back, seemingly unable to move, and I am above him, and I see her blood, dried on the ground, a beautiful sienna, spreading out like autumn leaves.

His wife had asked me, *what are you doing here,* because she knew this was possible.

"You're a married man," I say, thinking of the wrong I've done her.

He moves his neck like he's annoyed.

"Tell me how she died," I say, to change the subject.

"What do you mean?"

"I mean, how did Elena die? Tell me the details."

I can see him looking at me, his eyes slits. He pauses.

"Well, it was easy. I just bought a tombstone. No one asked any questions." Then he shakes his head. "Sam, that poor bastard."

"I don't remember," I say.

"The witness of the murder doesn't remember a thing! How fitting." Forester laughs and leans back. "Well, you were pretty far gone, I suppose. High in a tree, we didn't see you. Veranu had to go back, climb up there and get you. You had a roll of film in your hand. Wouldn't let go of it. That was amazing."

A light sweat breaks out on my body. Through the music I hear a camera shutter. I flinch and reach for the gold dress.

"What's the matter?" he asks, sitting up.

"I hear a camera."

"My god, you are one crazy chick." He lies back down, laughing.

"I heard it."

"So what? Let the ghosts take pictures."

My heart is racing, but I lean back down into the dirt and bunch the dress up under my head. Forester's hand glides up my body.

"What kind of perfume is that again?" he asks.

"How did you find us?" I ask.

"Um. Sam's idea. He knew her well, I guess. He was still drunk as shit too, running around, yelling at us to get in our cars and go looking for you two."

The cool air grips me, circling through my lungs. Forester's voice feels sinister. I can't breathe and my body stiffens as though I am frozen.

"Did you know them?"

"Who?"

"The poachers."

"The Wakamba? Their arrows are more effective than a heavy caliber gun. And yeah, I've met a few Somalis with G3s." He pauses, "But to know them is fluxional, an always transforming comprehension."

I consider this.

"So then," I say, "you knew them."

Forester stands up and holds out his hand, "Come on, the nights here can freeze you."

"No, leave me here," I answer. I cannot move anyway. The spell he seemed to cast over me is gone. He is no longer a stranger with inaccessible secrets. He is a part of the trap I'm in.

"Come on," he says. "I have some tequila in the house. That was Elena's favorite."

The pattern of the stars above me looks unfamiliar.

"Please," I say, "go away."

Forester disappears and I remain there naked for a while, and then I slowly get up, slip on the gold dress that smells of her perfume, that drapes me in drink, and I begin to dig with a rock, enraged and filled with frustration. I use both hands, the dirt pushing up under my fingernails. The ground is packed hard, and I work the rock until I have a hole in the ground as long as my forearm, as deep as my elbow. I have to pace myself or I won't finish. Obviously I need a shovel, so I stand up into the sky, a wave of darkness overtaking me for a moment, and then I run, hearing footsteps, toward the kitchen.

No shovel anywhere, but knives in the kitchen, and feeling a bit desperate, I grab the largest one. Forester is nowhere to be seen, but the music is so loud it thumps itself through my body. I return to the grave and chop at the damp earth with the knife, scooping it up with my hands, throwing it to the side. It seems I do this forever, but the music lasts forever too.

The coffin is impossibly deep in the ground, and impossibly long. But finally I can touch it, a cold wooden box. I make several attempts to pry open the lid and then walk around for a while in the cool air, catching my breath, watching the light come up. In one moment, out of silence, there is a sudden and deafening squawking of birds and insects. The sweat dries on my back and I shiver.

I am tired of the box and the dirt and my past and Forester. But I think of Elena, who used to lie in the sun, tanning, waiting for fire. That was the whole point of her drinking, to feel the alcohol light her body on fire. Forester had just told me what she wanted, which is something I had never realized. She wanted out.

I gather rough sticks and wood scraps from beyond the trees and bark and dried grass and throw them along the casket. I run inside. I grab Forester's bag of dope and cigarettes along with his lighter, which is what I was after, and two newspapers and two boxes of kitchen matches. I carry them out, sprinkle them all over, and light the whole mess. At first it looks like the fire won't take, but after what seems like a long while, the smoke stings my eyes and burns my throat and the flame flares up, steady and strong and a strange fluorescent yellow orange. The night is cold, I realize only after the warmth hits me. The night is freezing, in fact, and I warm my face and hands and feet, the fire reaching out toward the larger orange glow on the horizon. There are smells that come and go with the wind, a musty damp ammonia smell, and finally, burning wood.

And then I hear her voice through the fire. *Listen to me,* she says, *run.* So that the fire is something I can't stop the wave of; something alive I can never escape from.

And already, here and there, are bits of ash, gray and black, flinging themselves out of the fire, landing on me. A relocation of atoms.

I walk through the ashes. Run where? Where was I supposed to run?

This time I hear the footsteps before sensing them. I am alone with her finally—she always acts as though nothing has happened—and then he is behind me, breathing hard, yelling.

"*What the hell are you doing?*" Forester is sweaty and shaking and pouring sand on the fire. "What in the *hell* . . . ?" He is dancing around as though his feet hurt. I am vaguely amused, seeing him lose his cool.

"I saw the smoke from my room. You're insane. Pour dirt. Pour dirt." He kicks the thin dust at his feet into the hole and then runs back to the house.

I am waiting for her smile, the smooth wave of her voice, her body moving through space, slightly off balance. She will rise up, laughing at the idea of being buried in Africa. Laughing at the idea of being *shot*, right as she was gathering her most important photos.

"STOP the fire," he yells. "HELP me stop it." He returns with more dirt and appears genuinely angry. His face is distorted in the flames and the shadows of the early light. "STOP the fire." He is on his way back to the house for more sand. I hover on the edge of her grave and listen.

Run.

Forester arrives with a small fire extinguisher and more sand. His eyes are black. He's probably still drunk and stoned too. But he manages to single-handedly get the fire under control.

I've only seen someone shoot up once. I guess I'm a little out of it. Wayne Morrow was a casual friend of Michael's, and we had arranged to borrow his acetylene torch because Michael wanted to break apart and weld together an old iron gate he had found. We were in a hurry and illegally parked, so I went alone up the stairs to Wayne's apartment. The door was ajar and he was expecting us, so I tapped lightly and went in. In the center of his room, Wayne had just finished wrapping a rubber hose around his bicep, his long legs spread out before him. The vein on the inside of his arm was bulging, and when the needle slid in some blood spurted out. He was using his teeth to keep the rubber hose tight, and after he released it his head fell backwards, in a kind of relief and ecstasy, looking at the ceiling, and when he lifted his head again, a few seconds later, his arm was still bloody and I was standing there. Wayne looked pissed off when he saw me and I could almost see him trying to control what was about to become rage. He's about 6'3" and could have, without even trying, swung his arm and knocked my head off, but I was in the middle of a quick excuse, and as I asked him where the torch was, I also casually asked him what the hell happened to his arm. He dug into his pocket, his eyes an intense flame of blue, and then for the first time, as he pointed toward his kitchen, I noticed the tracks, small holes in his tanned and muscled arms, and I followed the veins in his arms with my eyes up to his face, and in his face I could see the life that had been freed, for the moment, to be the way it was, without the hindrance of the body or mind.

And for one moment I feel like this, at the edge of her partially burned and no-longer grave. There is about to be nothing in my way. Nothing will stop me now, the way nothing can stop you when you're young, before you know what can happen, before you know that chance, accident, fate, or mistakes actually exist, before you know that your greatest happiness might be taken away, or that you might get off track, that you might never achieve your dreams.

Forester kicks dirt back onto the coffin, his movements quick, precise, nervous.

"Take me to where she died," I say.

He squints at me, "What?"

"I want to go back there."

There is a pause. He seems to mouth at me, "are you mad?" though it is dark and difficult to see his mouth. Then he shrugs, a piece of Michael dismantled. He shakes his head.

"Well, it's far into Tsavo. It was closed to the public even then. Still is. You were in a woodland area by the river, just above Cloud Falls, and not long after you were there a couple of people were killed by lions."

"But the place is still there."

"There was a fire near there. It's probably unrecognizable."

"I'd still like to go."

"The poachers are worse now than they ever were," he says. "Now they want live animals, babies, elephant hide. It's like entering a war zone."

He takes my hand and pulls me toward the house, looking at the ground as he walks.

In the kitchen he leans against the cabinet, one shoulder up, the other down. He is waiting for water to boil, for tea.

"But yeah," he says, after the longest pause, "we could probably manage to get there."

He takes down two teacups and places them on the long wooden table.

"Your mother was a focused woman," he says, "ruthless in that."

"What do you mean?"

He sniffs the air, "I smell it, I can smell blood. I knew it the moment I saw her."

"But you're probably like that," I say.

He laughs rough, until he starts coughing. He pours the water from the kettle and hands me a cup of tea. It's yellow-green and tastes like lime.

"You never were like that," he says, "even as a kid."

"I can be like that, I can be ruthless."

"Never," he says. "You'll never be."

He walks away with his tea, toward his bedroom, and probably to prove him wrong, I get up and rummage through all the drawers in the kitchen. Perhaps another knife will open the coffin, though I also look for a screwdriver and a hammer. Near the back of a kitchen drawer I find a black-handled knife, circled with red rings. I push an almost invisible button, and a seven-inch blade shoots out. It surprises me so much that I drop it, a snake spinning and hissing on the floor. I kick it, then retrieve it, and return to the grave. I feel immune to the night while I hold the knife. I exit the house, and I am a part of the night, a part of another world, far enough into darkness to not see it and not care.

I walk quickly to the gravesite and leap in. More than half covered after Forester's work, I scoop out the loose dirt and ash with my hands until I am back to the bare wood of the coffin. The dirt smells of clay and burned wood. The cover is sealed, badly charred but not burned all the way through. I take the knife and concentrate on prying open the lid. It is an old casket and it won't open. Then, under the rim, I can feel two steel pins. The shifting of the bolts is so loud it startles me, but I turn them and push, and they unlatch.

Run. Run now.

I slowly lift the lid.

Look, I say to myself, I can be what Forester claims I am not—ruthless. She will feel the air. This will be her death. When she died, she sucked the breath out of me. This will be the end of my emptiness and sorrow and the end of all things.

There is a loud humming sound, and even with the sun forever about to rise, the available light doesn't show anything except a glowing series of lines. I find the lighter, still on the edge of the grave, and hold its small round spot of light onto a faded and dark velvet, torn in places, and the contents: a dirty and scraped-up tusk, the length of the coffin, about six feet, the tip beaten and rounded. And two femur bones, a skull, a pelvis bone, beside the tusk, around the tusk, in no particular order. The tusk is humming, vibrating the ground.

Maybe the long sound waves stay in the ivory. The long sound waves hum. Or maybe the humming is coming from across the yard. At any rate I can't hear anything except humming.

I pause for a moment, because Elena would have liked this, to be buried in ivory.

I know she can hear the humming. Especially since it is getting louder. It seems to be getting louder in direct proportion to the sun as it escapes from the dark horizon, the sun as it opens its throat to scream.

See what happens, Michael said to me one afternoon, as he trapped the Melanoplus differentialis in his palm. When the grasshopper spit red saliva I told him to let it go. This is the interesting part, Michael answered. Michael, who is good at identification and memorization, who does not like conjecture or metaphor. The grasshopper had screamed at him, and he ignored it.

She never looked back as she walked; she assumed I would follow. She assumed that doubt presupposes certainty; she knew nothing at all.

The wind shifts. I feel it shift on my arms and neck. I look around, slowly, to see about the humming.

There is a man walking toward me. He walks slowly, cautiously, bent a little forward like he's tracking something. I don't recognize him. I calculate how long it will take for me to get to the kitchen door. He straightens his back a little as he gets closer to me. He is coming straight at me and looking at me and I don't like it. I panic. I don't like him looking at me like that. There is a scream deep in my chest that I am pushing down. I drop the coffin lid and I half-walk, half-run, in an arc, toward the house. He crosses over in a radius to meet my arc.

"Jambo," he says, his accent heavy, his face damp and round.

Every cell in my body is screaming, and I begin to run; I am just taking off when he leaps at me, his craggy hand gripping my upper arm.

"Listen to me," he says. "It is about the lion."

He smells like licorice and sweat. I glance at the hand that is holding my arm and it has only three fingers. Without thinking, I twist my arm up and around and run toward the pink disc on the horizon.

I slam through the side door by the kitchen, and run past the zebra skin couch to my room. I am running down the hallway when I see myself in the mirror at the end of the hall. I feel huge spikes sticking out of the wall—pointed, razor-sharp spikes. I have to slow down to avoid them. And then my image is clearer. The gold dress is the same as being naked, and there are people before me, crumpled bodies at the base of the mirror.

I turn from the mirror and stand, breathing hard, in the doorway of my room. I'm facing the photographs Elena took years ago that I have taped to the wall. But in my mind I see the zebra skin couch that I just passed and Forester sitting there, legs folded, smirking, surrounded by the humming. I turn around and go out into the hallway. The mirror is behind me. The mirror only kills you if you look at it. It doesn't matter that I've already died hundreds of times. I can feel its pull; it wants me to look around again. It will kill me this time for sure. I resist, and walk into the living room. Forester sits in front of me, swinging his leg on the couch, smirking.

The damp round face appears in the kitchen doorway. He scuttles in, quickly, considering one foot drags. He looks deranged.

The humming is on the stereo; it is on AUX rather than CD. It is a hollow empty video noise, so loud it hurts my ears.

Forester grabs my wrist as I stand there, trying pull me down to the couch.

"Sit, there is someone I want you to meet."

I feel as though I've seen him before but I don't know who he is. And I'm hoping, for some reason, that he doesn't recognize me. There is sometimes no relationship between a young face and an old face, even on the same person. Especially between a child's face and the face they will become. Especially lately, I seem to have blue circles under my eyes. I think, I'll cover my face and he won't recognize me.

"Elena," Forester says, gripping my wrist more tightly as I try to pull away from him, "this is Veranu. He is our groundskeeper, you remember? He's been with me over twenty years."

The video AUX noise is humming so loudly I feel like I'll lose my hearing. I realize who I'm looking at.

There is a photo of Veranu in Elena's suitcase. He was much younger, standing beside the Land Rover, a semiautomatic slung over his shoulder, at the scene of the first elephant culling I witnessed.

He was someone we knew well. He loaded the guns and cleaned them on the porch afterward, smelling of that distinctive oil they use to clean guns, not unlike WD-40. He drove the trucks used for catering and laundry, and handled the liquor and kegs. The white of one of his eyes always had a large visible vein, one of the reasons I always found him hard to look at.

It is the same man standing before me now. He had been there for the cullings, for the parties, and he was there that morning at 5:00 A.M. when Elena was out taking photos of an elephant massacred at the hands of poachers. But he was not one of us then, he was in disguise, as a poacher, wearing his tan bandanna.

Elena fell first forward and then to the side in a kind of dance, a look of mystery on her face. A man ran over, and then another. The first one grabbed both cameras from around her neck; the second had his gun slung over his shoulder. And then angry voices, calling back and forth to each other in Swahili, the man with the tan scarf draped over his round face, his voice coming around the elephant. I knew his face even then, but I didn't recognize it, the situation didn't make any sense.

Later, after Sam ran onto the scene, after the gunshots, in the stillness, out of the stillness, in the rustling frenzied howling, as spotted long-necked bodies tore apart the already dismantled elephant, I realized that I had seen something I shouldn't have. But I couldn't exactly identify my forbidden knowledge, so that in my mind there is just a shadow of motion, in the way Elena fell forward, in the way Sam's head fell back, in the slouch of a man who cares for nothing, beneath the tree looking up at me, the act of a man who knows nothing of love.

And I'm looking at him now. The same round face, the eyes dark and unblinking. A survivor.

"The lion told me—" he utters, his voice thick.

I want to walk away, but Forester is still holding my wrist, so I just look into the corner of the room instead.

"—that my son would die. I didn't listen. The lion told me I would need to save you. I didn't listen to that. But in the end, all the lion said was true. My son died. That morning. And I took you from the tree."

"You were a poacher," I say, glancing at him.

He does not look away from my face, though I am back to staring at the corner. I can feel his eyes.

"The elephants disappearing are not a big problem. What is a big problem is when Manu hadn't eaten in two days. He was three. His mother was squeezing water into his mouth with a cloth. That was more difficult than even his death. What is a difficulty is when Manu's mother was killed by Somali rebels on a bus. What is unpleasant is having this—" he holds up his mutilated hand in front of my eyes so that I have to look, "done to you because they think you are not good at keeping secrets. I know secrets. Elephants disappearing are not a big problem."

I look at him. "Why are you telling me this?"

"Because you act disrespectfully. You show me disrespect."

"How?"

But Veranu seems angry now, and more tired.

"You tell her," he says, the light falling out of his eyes as he turns and walks out, slamming the side kitchen door behind him.

"What's your problem?" Forester asks me.

When I was in the tree Veranu's round face floated below me, his eyes steady as he silently stood there, jamming his gun up at me, motioning me to come down. Eventually, he ran away, back behind where Elena had been. And later the snarling animals whipped blood around in circles, dragging long gleaming intestines through the dirt. When he came back he had ropes, and he climbed up the tree and forced me down. I feel like without knowing it, I've been in that tree by Cloud Falls my whole life.

Forester runs his hand up my arm.

I look at him and attack, hoping to tear open his flesh. He has misunderstood everything. He is a hyena, a cackling waste, and I make his face bleed and I will make it bleed more, so that his skin is gone, so that I see only cartilage. I am quick and strong, and Forester is old, but he is heavy and quick too, talking low, pinning me down, his face bleeding down my neck.

I'm still wearing the skin-tight gold dress, covered in dirt and sweat. The urge to kill him is gone.

"All right," I rasp out.

He says nothing, but I can hear him breathing on me, his blood dripping onto my skin. Time passes.

There is a knocking at the door.

His arms tighten around me slowly, like a boa constrictor.

"Stay out," Forester yells.

Forester has had malaria off and on and I wonder if I'll catch it. He rubs his hand over the blood on his face and runs his hand over my arms.

We lie like that a few days, a few hours. I wouldn't know, because all days are now one matted together. One day. One life. One moment. One breath.

"Who murdered Sam?" I ask.

"How do you know that Sam is dead?"

"Because Sam is dead."

"How do you know anything at all? You were nine."

"Are you saying that Sam isn't dead?"

"I'm saying that to facilitate your understanding of the esoteric areas of the past, or the present, you need to keep in mind that things are rarely what they appear to be at first glance."

How annoying he is.

"As if I don't know that," I quip.

"Elena very much loved Sam, for example."

"Then why did she leave him?" I ask.

"She needed more," he says.

"That's not love."

"It could be. Love is complicated," he says, "and anyway, love keeps people alive."

"Real love is not complicated."

"Maybe it's the most complicated," he says.

"Well, if Sam's not dead where is he?"

Forester smirks. "Well, let's invite him for dinner. Veda knows his number. She'll fix something special."

"Who's body is in the coffin with the tusks?"

Forester clenches and unclenches his arms.

"Veranu's son. Thus your disrespect."

I'm a little shocked by this. But I decide to move on.

"Why did you make a gravestone for Elena?"

"You could take that casket with the tusk to America if you want. I have the paperwork."

"The paperwork is fake; what if I get caught?"

He shrugs. "The paperwork looks real. Anyway, you would just pay them off."

"I don't think that answers my question."

"Which question?"

"About the gravestone."

"Oh right. Well, she knew too much, had seen too much. It was safer for her if her wounds were fatal. You know that. You watched me put the flowers on her grave. Anyway, it's kind of nice. It keeps her close."

I have forgotten why he is pinning me down. I have not slept; I spent the night finding ivory and Veranu's son in a coffin. I don't fully understand a word he's saying. And realizing this, after believing it all, I look at him.

"Let me up," I say.

"Not yet."

"Now."

He is hurting my back, and I am about to twist away from him, but his arm lifts, and after the heavy weight of it is up I find I can breathe again. I roll away from his smirking face.

"Veranu rescued you, that day," he says.

"He also killed my mother," I answer, and walk to the drawer in the kitchen where the switchblade had been. There was another knife in there that would do in an emergency. I'm thinking that nothing was the way he says it was. "Was he working for you?" I ask. "It must have irritated you that Sam showed up."

I'm standing with my back to the drawer, my hand on the handle, ready to get the knife.

"No. Veranu didn't shoot her. But the guy in the coffin—Veranu's son—he shot her. Thank god it was a gun and not one of his poison-tipped arrows. If he hadn't shot her someone else would have, and fatally. He probably knew exactly what he was doing. He was an incredible shot. The ivory is your mother's, by the way. A gift from Veranu. The ivory is in exchange for Sam's life. A commanding price, usually they call it even with a cow or two."

"How did Veranu's son die?"

"Manu. He was standing in the wrong place at the wrong time. Someone from our troop hit him."

I sink down against the kitchen cabinet and onto the floor. It finally dawns on me who Manu was. Manu worked on the other side of the property, but I would see him around the house on his day off. I used to read him Andy Capp comics and watch as he prepared his poisons. He used to dip his arrows in glasses filled with different colored liquids, usually brown or green, but sometimes yellow, and twice he let me come with him to time the death of the rabbits and frogs that crossed his path. His favorite poison was something he took from tree bark, called Muriju, and once I was with him when he collected it. I never knew that Manu was Veranu's son, and I never knew that Manu had died that day. He was about seventeen and famous for being good with a bow and arrow. He talked to me on our walks. *You are silent, silent is good,* he would say, in his thick accent. *Arrows are silent. The sky is silent. And if you hunt hard enough, even the mosquitoes are silent; you can't feel them when they bite.*

With Manu, I didn't mind watching the animals die. If I had known back then that Manu had died, I would have never forgiven my mother.

"And what did Elena give to Veranu in exchange for Manu's life?" I ask Forester.

But just then the phone rings, and when Veda starts speaking on the machine, Forester stands up, grabs the phone from the living room, and walks down the hall, leaving me alone on the kitchen floor, sitting in front of a drawer with a knife in it.

After a while I pick up the phone in the kitchen. It's the old kind that has a circle you dial. The black handle is incredibly heavy. I'm surprised there's a dial tone. I dial Elena's number, a painfully laborious process, half expecting someone else to answer, or for the number to not exist, or not work.

I don't know what time it is there, but she answers after a few rings.

"I think he's alive," I say. "Sam is alive."

"What?"

"Sam is coming for dinner."

"Sam is dead, honey. If there's anything left of Sam it's his ghost. I put him on the plane myself, back to his mother in Washington, DC."

"But Forester said—" I begin.

I can hear her breathing. For the first time in years.

She interrupts, "Forester is crazy, which you must remember. Forester does not live in the real world. You cannot believe anything he says. He's dangerous in that way."

"But maybe—"

"Maybe nothing," she says, and hangs up.

She is always hanging up on me.

I mill around the kitchen. The counters are cool to touch, cream-colored tiles, chipped on the edges, a little dirty in the cracks. The label on the hand soap is French, the dish soap is Joy, in English. The field outside is turning blue with the rising sun, and my brain is flashing footage: more than 2,000 confiscated tusks piled high in a barbed wire lot in Nairobi, burning as a statement against ivory trade. The sky is alive with ash. Manu is sitting on his kitchen floor, at the age of three, with nothing to eat. And I am stuck, trapped, caught in a web that has no entrance and no exit.

6

I really can't believe she hung up. I replace the phone. There is a way in which a witness is not a passive person but an active one; they are an externalization of the event. He called me the witness of the murder. And then he claimed there was no murder.

In order to remember something, you must: one) perceive that something is happening; two) store the information in several different places in the brain depending on which and how many sensory stimulations take place; and three) retrieve the information. If something profoundly shocking happens, usually the memories reenact themselves without any conscious effort—just as TV sports give us instant replays, our minds do the same thing with traumatic memories, replaying them over and over.

I never actually saw the images until I met Michael. I had felt the same sudden onset of anxiety, randomly, perhaps as I passed a stranger wearing Chanel No. 5, or at the worn look in someone's eye, or in a certain moment of some innocuous song—at these moments I paused, as though if I were to move I would black out; I would look away and wait for it to pass. But I never saw images. The images came with Michael; they arrived as my mind crossed over from consciousness to pure body, cessation of mind.

But after a while I began seeing images just standing in his presence, especially if he happened to use some phrase that also happened to be a part of a song. So that the words, *I don't know why*, would take me immediately into the abyss. Whether true or not, I imagine Jagger knows what he is doing, when he lets go for that second. Mick is an actor; he puts on a good show; he always seems like he's letting go when in fact that's just a part of the show. But every now and then, Mick is a part of the enigma of music, where it exists beyond the musician himself, so that he releases his life, sacrifices it for the music, if only for a moment, and so also when Sam looks at heaven instead of around him, when he releases his body just before he is forced to let it go—he is telling Elena that he loved her. I am a witness to Sam's release. It ends as his body jerks backwards over Elena's when the bullet rips him apart. Through the shuffling and yelling and activity I keep my eyes on them, until they are eventually dragged away, their hands scraping the red earth.

Sam and Elena work in the emergency room. The nights when she is on call and can't get a babysitter, I accompany her to the hospital. She finds an empty operating room that smells like formaldehyde where I'm supposed to sleep. The smell makes me feel weak. In the moonlight I trace with my eyes the beds equipped with tubes and tanks that carry a life force more powerful than my own blood and veins. One night, Sam and Elena rush into the room, assuming that I am asleep. They laugh and bang against the wall that pulses with silver moonlight, their laughter quickly turning into deep and heavy breathing.

I imagine that the moment Sam looks into Elena's eyes he sees his death, but he mistakes it for sex. That's how sex and death are related, in that they are easily confused.

Sam and Elena are married on a beach in Tahiti. I stay with my father during their honeymoon, and he tells me he's still in love with my mother and always will be. I feel terrible for him. But when Elena returns I move into Sam's house with her. My friends make fun of Sam because he wears faded jeans and woven shirts from Guatemala and African necklaces. But Elena is happy—she loves the way Sam can sit down and spontaneously play Bach's *Goldberg Variations;* that he graduated from Harvard; that he travels everywhere; is published in medical journals; and speaks German, French, Chinese, and Italian. She is impressed, in love, and everything is bliss until we move, a year after their wedding, to Bamako, Mali.

Sam's work in Bamako involves training Peace Corp volunteers to give general medical help to the locals, and Elena does this as well, working in the office as a nurse, but Sam also wants her to document several of his patients—and he has brought along a big, metal Nikon for this—so Elena begins taking photographs that provide Sam with data and evidence for his work.

Sam stays out in the field for weeks at a time. He travels on back roads around West Africa, and because of the travel conditions, the civil wars, the starvation and cholera, he doesn't want us to join him. He introduces Elena to his friends at the American Embassy and to the other doctors in town, and leaves us on our own. Elena hates it when he leaves, partly because in spite of daily French lessons, she still has difficulty understanding everything and her pronunciation is erratic. Sam rarely calls us from the road, saying that he is often in places where there is no phone. My only real interaction with Elena is during dinner, when we sit at the table and eat silently. I watch the lizards, and Elena doesn't actually eat, she drinks whiskey instead.

Soon, Elena doesn't go into the office at all; she spends her time driving around looking for something to photograph.

One evening, after Sam has just returned from a long trip, we are driving back from dinner at a friend's house. Sam is driving as fast as he can through a closed-down market area. It is dark, and the litter-strewn space is muddy and filled with deep potholes.

"You have to *try*, Elena," Sam says through clenched teeth. "They don't talk to you because you don't let them."

"Because they don't care about what's important," she interrupts. "These people are *hungry*, they can't even feed their children. No, they're not hungry. They're *starving*."

"On average, Elena, they have *sixteen* children. *I* couldn't feed sixteen children."

Sam accelerates through the dips and ditches and my head hits the side window. Our headlights shine crookedly off the road, and we see a light-brown body leap up before us, fall and bounce like a ball for a few feet, until landing like a rag doll. Elena screams, and Sam argues. Finally he stops the car and turns it around to illuminate the pale, lifeless body of an animal.

Elena is gripping my arm, pulling me out of the car and through the dark, past the body, back into the market.

"It's just a dog!" Sam yells. "Do you know what I've *seen*? Do you know what *matters*?"

Sam bangs something on the hood of the car and yells after us, "Besides, this isn't starvation. This is hungry. Starvation looks different. And starvation is easy compared to what else these people go through."

I run to keep up with her as she blends into the darkness with her ever-darkening tan. The darkness swallows her with a great inhalation, and I am alone, a ghost in the marketplace: small, pale, unknown.

One afternoon Elena and I are walking from our house to the American Embassy. It has just rained and there are hundreds of small toads covering the dirt roads. I bend down and catch them, filling up a pouch I make with my t-shirt. The air is warm and clean, the frogs jumping all around our legs, and then we hear hooting, yelling, and three teenage boys emerge from behind a fence. A ball of mud splats onto my chest. Another hits my face. I'm not scared, just confused. I look over at Elena and expect her to yell at them. But she walks by, standing tall, and even when a mud ball hits her on the back, she remains absolutely silent, ignoring them, deliberately slowing down even as they run into the street behind us, yelling insults and throwing toads, the little things crawling around my neck, getting caught in my hair.

At the embassy, *Gone with the Wind* is playing on a screen wide across the sky. We clean the mud off in the bathroom. It is a barbecue, and everyone mingles around, talking and laughing.

Elena hardly speaks to anyone.

"Get yourself some chicken," she tells me, swirling her drink.

I ignore her and watch the movie.

"Sam's friends don't think I'm good enough for them," she says, "since I don't speak French and didn't graduate from Harvard."

Then the houses on screen are on fire, and the girl in the red dress is frantic, and Elena is laughing hysterically and singing "Delta Dawn," to herself, so that anyone sitting nearby is watching her instead of the movie.

Sam has been gone for twenty-one days. We have not heard from him in twelve. Elena is alternately enraged, drunk, impassive. One afternoon I'm on top of the house, walking around in the wet laundry that hangs from ropes spread from tree to tree across the roof. A French boy next door yells *le pleu, le pleu,* but the sun continues to shine as huge drops of rain fall from the sky. I hold my hands out to catch the rain, each drop lit from within, a small sun. The raindrops are beautiful, but Elena is calling my name, and in her voice I hear the end of the world.

On my way down the stairs everything is yellow: butter flowers, speckled frogs, faded mustard lizards with sticky feet.

She is standing in the driveway that curves and extends itself into the patio.

"We are leaving on a trip to the desert," she says. "Go pack."

I tell her that a second kitten has drowned in our algae-filled pool; the gardener found it last night.

"So, *stop* giving them your milk. You make the cook angry because he could give that milk to his children."

"But the kittens are also starving," I tell her, "and now the cook will have no one to cook for."

"Just go pack."

And that afternoon, just before we leave, I place a big bowl of milk next to the crumbling wall and cracked green pool, oblivious to the danger I am creating for the kittens.

It is a long bus ride to the Niger River. Once there, we embark on a boat that will take us to Timbuktu. Elena says that maybe we will find Sam and maybe we won't, but we'll at the very least be having an adventure of our own. The river doesn't move, except for a few eddies swirling in the light brown water. Our already overflowing boat pulls two completely crowded barges filled with people packed in so close that everyone is touching. It is hot. I play cards on the floor of the cabin.

Four days later Elena trades cigarettes and underwear for camel rides into remote camps.

Then, in a whitewashed hut in Timbuktu, Elena discovers her camera doesn't work. It is filled with sand, just like the bread, the water, the dried fish.

A man from Georgia takes a Polaroid of me sitting on a camel. Almost frantically, Elena tries to trade something for his camera. The man refuses, but snaps one more Polaroid of me and hands it to Elena before moving on. She is angry that I like my Polaroids. She yells so much that I run out, into the dunes, the sun so bright I can't see the sky. My legs sink into the sand that moves all around me in a long sweeping eternal wind so that I run, hot as light, into the shimmering blue ocean of sand, immune to her fire of words, the sand nothing to conquer now.

Toads bigger than my fists jump into my legs as I walk. When finally I return to the hotel, Elena is in the bathroom, desperately cleaning her camera, and when it still doesn't work, she takes it apart piece by piece as though tearing apart its limbs, throwing it into the trash can next to the toilet. Roaches swarm the bathroom, and within a few hours they have all nestled into her camera, filling its thin crevices.

Elena believed that her photographs were about documenting real-ity and truth. That the reality and truth of events could be altered by photographing or not photographing them, I don't think ever occurred to her.

I see her from across the room. She sits below a fan in the lobby of the hotel. I'm afraid the fan will fall on her and I'll be left here all alone. She orders a vodka and water but they bring her some-thing else. I'm on the other side of the room; she needed space. I'm supposed to be quiet and nice. Just as her hair falls from its leather tie, tumbling in auburn past her shoulders, a man walks up to her, leans onto the bar, a drink in his hand. She laughs in that funny way, trembling in the shade he casts over her rising breasts.

His name is Forester, and he buys us dinner that night, and after dinner, I sleep on the floor while hundreds of cockroaches file around and over the tiles I sleep on, over my legs and sheet, emerg-ing in swarms from the drains in the bathroom, intent on march-ing straight into my bed.

"They won't hurt you," Forester says.

The next morning I find him sitting outside on the patio. His shirt is ironed a bright white, and he smells like cologne. He is drinking coffee.

"How would you like to see a giraffe, out in the wild, or an ele-phant?" he asks.

"It won't be fun for her unless she can send a photo back," I tell him. "Her camera broke."

"Nonsense. It will be quite fun."

Elena enters the patio looking more tan than ever, sheathed in the shimmering thin gold cloth that shows every curve.

"Put your hat on," she tells me, sitting on his lap.

"Your daughter here was telling me you need a camera to enjoy the elephants."

She laughs in that way again, her neck exposed to his mouth, then she looks at me, "Why don't you go catch some more frogs while Forester and I talk?"

"They're toads," I tell her. And already two of my toads had died, and she knew that, so instead I bury the one Polaroid of me I can find deep in a sand dune on the side of the hotel.

Forester Ecco is rich. More wealthy than Sam Fraizer would ever be. He found West Africa to be boring, and thought we should go with him to Kenya. Kenya is where everything happens, he says. Kenya is a magic land, and you can speak English. So, of course, Elena agrees.

We live with Forester for several months. He spends his time with wildlife biologists, flying over the landscapes and counting elephants. He takes photographs of the drought and its devastation, of the wars in nearby countries. He knows journalists, artists, models, rock stars, doctors, scientists, businessmen—everyone. He is on the Board of Wildlife Management, and that was how we all went out culling one day. The elephant family was wasting away, on the brink of starvation.

About seven months after we arrive at Forester's ranch, I am playing jacks on the porch, smelling the hot tar as a road crew pours asphalt on the main highway about a half mile away, when a ragged-out Peugeot comes up the drive. Sam steps out of the car.

I run over to meet him. "Sam!"

"Yeah," he says, distracted. "This car's taken apart half the road." He points to his tires, lined thick with wet asphalt and tar. Then abruptly, "Where's Elena?"

"Inside."

I follow him in.

Elena is lounging at the kitchen table, listening to the BBC, painting her nails white.

She looks up. "Ohmygod . . . Sam."

"Hello."

"What are you doing here?" She seems both happy to see him and annoyed at the same time, if that's possible.

"Well," Sam sighs, "I miss you. I'm still wearing a ring. It means something to me. It was a promise."

"A promise of what?" Elena asks, bristling. "Some act of fidelity? I hadn't even heard from you in twelve days."

Sam shrugs. "Elena, what is twelve days? Nothing. A blip. You know I was working. I was in transit. It wasn't possible to contact you."

Elena has a habit I know well. Anytime I want to talk to her she distracts herself, so that she delays and deadens the conversation. She gets up to swat a fly, or pour the boiling water for her tea. She makes a production of wringing out the bag, stirring honey into her tea, tapping the spoon against the cup, laying the spoon down, and then there is the fly again, in the midst of my sentence, her part of the conversation reduced to, uh-huh, uh-huh, while she misses the fly, and then picks up the spoon again, moving the tea bag over.

She does this to Sam as he stands there, turning up and down the volume on the radio, sliding her sandals across the floor, playing with the lid on the nail polish bottle.

"Would you like some tea?" she asks him.

"I was *working*, Elena, you know that," Sam repeats. "Often there was no phone available."

"Well, one day in Bamako without you seemed like an eternity, and anyway, I've been working too," she says.

Sam cracks his knuckles. "Elena, you have nothing here. You were doing important work for me."

"No, I wasn't. All those photos were the same. I'm taking great, newsworthy photographs now. And Forester is sending them out. He knows people."

"Well, look," Sam cranes his neck from side to side and then takes his hands and cracks his neck, "I love you and would like you to come back."

Elena seems to still be listening to the radio.

"I'm not coming back until I achieve something, Sam. Until I can stand in front of your Harvard friends and say *fuck you*."

"Elena—"

"And how did you find this place?"

"Word eventually gets around."

Just then Forester walks out of his darkroom with several dripping wet photographs in his hands. When his drying screens are full, he uses the refrigerator and the windowpanes to let them dry, just slapping them up there.

"Who's this?" Forester asks, glancing at Sam as he walks to the refrigerator.

Elena is pushing back her cuticles, "Oh, this is Sam Fraizer. And Sam, this is Forester Ecco."

"Pleased," Sam says.

"Likewise." Forester stands there with that same smirk on his face that he gets after shooting elephants, smoothing his wet photos onto the freezer.

"I've just come to discuss something with Elena," Sam says.

"Like a drink?" Forester asks.

"No, thank you."

"Warm up for the party tonight. Where'd you fly in from?"

"Bamako."

Elena and Sam have been married for about a year and a half. I have never seen them fight. When Sam gets mad he just walks away.

"Elena, can we take a walk?"

"Okay," she says, and stands, her sandals loose around her feet so that she has to fix them again.

After they leave the room, Forester disappears again into his darkroom, so I go outside and watch the cooks set out four linen-covered tables around one side of the yard. They bring in catered food from Nairobi and serve it on colored porcelain plates, but I never eat anything except Hershey's chocolate milk powder mixed into peanut butter, both items available all over Africa, it seems.

Late that afternoon, when I come back after popping tar bubbles at the edge of the driveway, Sam is alone, his car parked next to the house in the sun, under the window of the library. The hood of the car is up and he's working on the engine. He looks like a guy you would find in a Greek ruin, hunched over the weeds that grow up over fallen columns, searching for coins buried in dust.

"Sam," I say, "I'll help you."

He looks at me with watery eyes and cocks his head toward the library window overlooking his car. "Shhhhh," he says, looking at me solemnly.

I don't hear anything.

He is taking out the air filter and pulling out the spark plugs.

Sam almost never does anything without listening to the news.

"Why isn't the radio on?" I ask.

"Shhhhhhh. I told you. Damn it."

Then I hear the sound, from the window, a woman's voice, sticky and caught. It is a sound I do not know the meaning of, a slow and continuous, *Ooooh God,* so I leave Sam to go in to investigate. I walk to the front of the house and open the screen door lightly, careful not to let it slam.

The knob is broken on the library door. I push it open. It looks more like evening in the room with the shades drawn. Elena half sits up from the lion skin, naked, and Forester lifts his head, glances at me, and then drops his head back onto the floor.

"Sam's working on his car," I tell them. My mother's hand travels up Forester's thigh. He pulls her back down to him, locks her nakedness onto his with his leg.

"So go help Sam with his car," Elena says, her voice muffled.

I stand in the doorway watching them, feeling afraid. I look up at a painting on the wall. The painting looks exactly like them, except it shows a tablecloth with a shadowy vase and pears.

"I want to hear a record," I say.

"Forester and I are sleeping. Go away."

"I want to hear a record," I repeat, knowing I should disappear but not being able to.

Forester is holding my mother's hair with one hand and kissing her on the mouth. I shut the door and return to Sam. His eyes are still watery, but he is sitting on the hood in the sun having a smoke.

"Can I try it?" I ask.

"No," but he flips the butt casually across his fingers to hand it to me, the same playful way he would have handed it to Elena.

This is really the beginning of our alienation, Elena's and mine. I feel I need to take sides, and I choose Sam, because he is sad, patiently waiting for her return. He is on the outside, with me. When Sam finally walks into the house, I make him some Tang, that orange drink you make from powder, and as he drinks it he quizzes me on my multiplication tables, just like he used to.

When Elena and Forester finally amble out of the library, Sam and I are waiting at the kitchen table. Sam cracks his neck and leans back in his chair.

"Car fixed?" Forester asks.

"It is," Sam answers.

Elena looks distant, and leaves the room to change her clothes.

Forester throws parties at least once a week, sometimes twice. Usually they are of two kinds: formal, where Forester hires musicians to play his old Steinway in the yard, along with other men and women dressed in black who bring cellos and violins and play everything, though Forester particularly likes Chopin and

Beethoven and Schubert. The pianist flutters his fingers over the keyboard and flips back his coattail in between long pauses in notes. On those nights the guests wear only suits or dresses, and Elena wears clothes that Forester has flown in for her.

The casual parties are augmented by the Rolling Stones and Donna Summer singing "Love to Love You Baby," and most people dance until dawn, their jewelry flashing, their colored nails holding crystal glasses filled with wine.

Tonight the party is an unusual mix, casual and fancy, rock records and a few musician friends, so Forester has the Steinway put in the center of his yard, but also has records piled up and ready around the turntable.

Multicolored pills sparkle in a cut glass bowl on the zebra skin table, and the speakers outside are cranked high enough so that you can just barely hear yourself talk.

Sam borrows a tuxedo from Forester, and they are smoking together in the living room just as the guests arrive.

I push my wet finger around the rim of a crystal glass so that the chime is endless if I put my ear close enough to hear it above the music. There is a little boy, younger than me, in a suit, swinging on my swing, sweeping it into full motion, the frayed knots screeching against a branch.

Elena is nowhere in sight. I find Sam swaying in front of the large silkscreen painting of Forester. It hangs in the library above the lion skin rug.

"Hi, Sam."

"Do you know what this is?" he asks me.

"It's Forester," I answer.

"No, it's a Warhol."

"A what?"

Sam touches the canvas with the tips of his fingers, "And that painting over there," he points, "the garden and trees, that's a Courbet, next to the mask."

Sam waves his arm about and walks out without saying anything else. I follow him, trying to be inconspicuous, and watch him grab a drink off the traveling silver tray. He walks around talking to different women. Then he finds Forester, accuses him of being an idiot, behind the times for playing *Let It Bleed* instead of *Let It Be,* which is obviously more sophisticated and intelligent music, not to mention more *ethical,* but Forester laughs at him and claps him on the shoulder and gets him another drink.

At dusk the crystal shines opalescent, and everything on the linen-covered tables wavers as though the tables themselves emanate heat. Elena finally appears on the scene, wearing the long white Dior with a slit up the side that hugs her hips and breasts. She is very tan, with a heart-shaped face and wide smile. She has a low, friendly laugh with an edge that Sam used to say made him feel as though she were tickling his neck. For a few minutes, Forester walks with his arm around her, then he moves on into the crowd.

And for a few minutes, I follow Elena. Her voice rises and falls with laughter and exclamations as she walks out onto the green lawn, chatting with various people. Then I sneak off to the fence near the edge of the grass where I am alone, where I can still hear the bass rhythm and main voice of the music, and for as long as I can, until I am completely out of breath, my feet shuffle and beat against the ground and my arms wave in the sky. I am the heat of the ground as it radiates up into darkness and I am the cool night air beating down. In the currents between the notes, when voices and laughter are not overtaking the sky, I can hear a date palm blowing in the breeze, the mosquitoes buzzing, and the occasional sound of an elephant.

When I am tired of dancing I just stand there. Then across the lawn I see Elena, a ghost of white, lighting her way toward the hot tub and beyond. I take off running and follow her, but somehow lose sight of her dress, her hat, the tilt of her head. I travel from the side of the house near the Acacia trees, the redwood deck where the hot tub is, and after being interrupted by an older man, who claims he can't tell the color of my dress in the darkness, with the colored lights, I walk around to the edge of the yard. And there she is again. I have anticipated by her walk that she's in her crazy mode, determined and happy. Tight, Sam calls it. I can't follow without being seen, so I run along the fence at the far edge and come up on her from the side. It takes a while and the music seems to pull me back and forth, so that when I finally see her whiteness, she is a luminous moth, dancing this way and that. She is waiting, and soon Forester stands before her, and in the moonlight I can see the silver African cross he wears, a cross with a fancy center and three points shooting off from that. I stand just beyond where the grass has been cut, whisking away mosquitoes, and watch the tilt of her moth-like figure bend down to his waist. Forester's face tilts to the sky and her hat flutters, bobbing to Jagger's, "I Don't Know Why," while AK-47s sound off beyond the fence.

When I turn around to go back, after they have left, I almost trip over Sam in the grass.

"What are you doing?" I whisper.

"I love your mother. She's a good woman," he says.

"Why?" I ask. "Why do you love her?"

"Help me up."

"Did you see them?" I ask.

"I see everything," he says, "I hear everything."

I would like to talk to him about something. I don't care what: viruses, long division, the Beatles versus the Rolling Stones. But he tells me it's time for me to be in bed, and then he throws himself into the crowd.

I sit down next to five adults gathered around a small glass table near the fountain. They are eating mango slices and drinking brandy. A few of them are Americans, and it is their little boy who had taken over my swing. He is asleep already, lying on a blanket in the grass under the stars and moon.

Someone is talking about the *musth* elephant. They say tonight someone will surely get him. The moon is almost full, just a sliver off. The local gossip lately has been about a lion nearby that killed a neighbor's dog, and the young male elephant in *musth*, his testosterone high so that in general everyone is trying to avoid him, but Forester says that if he acts up too much he'll get shot.

"I hear there's a whole group of them, and not just after the *musth* elephant either," someone says.

"What a mighty color," a woman says, "the yellow of a Hunter's Moon."

A man nearby overhears.

"Dying Grass Moon, dear. That's what we call it."

"And there, Venus is rising," she says. "You know what that means."

I have been sitting on a small bench, everyone around me a gray hazy glow, and then out of a lawn chair, Elena rises up, her white dress silent with velocity as she swaggers away toward the larger crowd nearer to the music.

When the music changes I go looking again for her. She is standing on the perimeter of the area where everyone dances. Her energy emanates in waves, and looking closely, her hair seems to have some fire in it, a burnt orange, a pale amber. But her eyes are impossibly pale in her tanned face, so that I almost think they aren't there.

"Love to Love You Baby" is playing again, and Elena is watching Sam through the darkness as he dances drunk and crazy with a woman. The woman's bare breasts are jiggling in and out of Sam's mouth while she pours champagne down her chest.

Forester appears out of nowhere and takes Elena's hand as she watches Sam.

"You won't break my heart," he says. "Go back."

"I will," she answers. "I will break your heart."

He has that smirk. "You won't."

And then Forester is mingling again, and Sam dances with a wineglass on his forehead, an amusing accomplishment, which everyone claps for.

I am standing just to the side, and I recklessly slide up beside her.

"Sam saw you," I say.

"What?" She is standing very straight, her eyes like a sponge, still looking to where everyone is dancing.

"And heard you. With Forester," I say.

She turns and slaps me hard across the face, but I feel the shame in my chest, my lungs burning as I breathe in her Chanel No. 5.

Later, she is sitting in the living room. The music is off, and a man next to the turntable is shifting through the records as though in a daze. As I walk by, Elena pulls me down next to her on the couch. Her eyes are fire-red where the whites usually are and she breathes fire into my face and takes my hand, reading my palm.

"You'll never be loved, see there? You have no heart line. No heart line means that you'll be just like me." She leans into me with her whiskey breath, the slit in her dress revealing her bare thigh, which is touching me, making me want to vomit.

I escape from her clutch. I am on my way to the bedroom where I sleep, but I hear music in the yard, so I step out the side door of the kitchen and into another world. The man who usually plays for hire is sitting at the piano, in the middle of the yard. He is not flashing his hands over the keyboard as he usually does, nor is he flipping back his coattail between pauses in notes. He is just playing, his hands like froth in the near dawn, his voice humming along with the music, sometimes so that the individual notes are obscured by his voice. As long as he is playing I know that nothing bad can happen, his music will save us all, and I go to sleep in a lawn chair near the piano.

He is not there when I wake up. Someone has thrown a sweater and some torn mosquito netting over me. The light is purple; everything is visible but shadowed. I'm freezing. I walk around to the front of the house. I'm on my way to the front door when I see a lion sitting on the hood of Sam's car. A male, looking right at me. A tremor rises up to my throat, although he is not moving, just twitching his tail against the side window. I can't decide whether I should go back or go forward, toward the house. He is looking right at me, and for one fleeting second I see myself tracking something, blood in the long grass to my right, fear in my belly, and then I look away. I take the five steps to the front door without looking at him, and walk slowly inside.

There are a few pills on the floor, and a man without a shirt asleep on the couch, but the servants have cleaned up everything else. I am about to go change into my white jeans and Raiders sweatshirt when I hear something fall. I go into the kitchen and there is Elena sneaking around, getting ready to go. She has changed her clothes, and is gathering up things around the house. Two cameras hang around her neck.

"Where are we going?"

"Shhhhhh," she insists.

Dark circles fall under her eyes. She is digging in the pocket of Sam's jacket in the entry hall.

"I heard something last night," she whispers. "In French, in Swahili, these men were talking . . . I need more film."

And then she is in the closet back by the darkroom where Forester keeps his film in a separate refrigerator.

The man passed out on the couch lifts his head. A shirtless man with dark hair.

"Where's Elena?" he asks.

And only then I realize it is Sam.

There is a lion on your car, I want to tell him, and Elena is going to drive away in it. She is leaving to take photographs of dead elephants. But I doubt he'll let her borrow his car for such a journey, and I doubt he will approve of her going. I do not want her plans to be ruined; I understand her passion.

I have hesitated; he must have seen me stall.

"I don't know," I say.

Sam accepts this, and sinks back into the couch with his eyes closed.

With my words I was supposed to protect her, and with those same words I betrayed who she loved—and thus betrayed her as well.

Only years later do I realize it's possible that Sam saw through me, chose to honor my surface statement, and later acted.

Elena walks through the living room and out the front door.

I run after her without saying anything, so that Sam will not lift his head.

She is walking toward Sam's car.

The light has changed already, and for several seconds I can't see her in the pink glare. I look to the hood of Sam's car. The lion is gone. Elena is opening the door.

She motions me back with her arms and puts her finger over her lips to tell me to be quiet, but I run and get in the passenger side.

"Go inside and pack," she whispers.

"Why?"

"We're going back to Bamako with Sam."

"I like it here."

Then she starts driving, down the asphalt road to the highway, on the highway and then off, and onto a small road, until finally we cross over onto bare land. We follow the faint trace of Land Rover tracks, and then the car is barely moving as the landscape changes. We drive for a long time, slowly, through tall grass, making our own tire tracks now, the car always about to get stuck.

When we finally get stuck, Elena's in a big hurry.

"Carry this," she says, throwing me the heavy bag. "Smell that? Massacre." She stalks forward, her dark arms swinging, her cameras hanging around her neck. I can see the pores of her face. I can see her eyes beyond the sunglasses she wears, the way they scan the ground in front of us. She pulls down branches, separates leaves. There are vines and spiderwebs everywhere.

"Be very quiet," she says. "Can't you walk faster?"

Practically running already, and nervous about the location, I just nod. The camera bag is heavy. I know we shouldn't be in the African wilderness without a guide or someone who can cover you if a lion or some other animal attacks, someone who knows what to do in an emergency. I had heard plenty of tales about rhinos and elephants and snakes—often harmless, but when provoked or angry, potentially deadly.

"We should have invited Forester," I say.

"Shhhhhh."

She scans the ground where an elephant has broken vines, flattened the ground with its large feet, a footprint I could sit down in and move around in easily. Later on, the leaves on both sides of us are smeared shiny with blood. And with the wind shifting, I am submerged in a sweet orange and metallic smell, dense enough to make me gag.

A few vultures circle overhead in a mild tornado pattern, about 300 feet in front of us.

"Let's go back," I say. "I know we should go back now."

"Come on, there are photos up ahead. Important ones. Be quiet."

A sudden scuttling through the branches, maybe a voice, and she stops, grabbing the camera bag from me and unzipping it. She takes out a handgun which I have never seen before and stands, unmoving, for several seconds. Even with all the noise of the land, all I hear is my heart pounding. She drops the gun into her front pocket and continues on until we are upon it. Larger than I ever imagined possible, a body looms before us, black and moving with flies, so many flies that the sky is hissing. Elena clicks away, unaware of anything except her photographs. She shoos away flies, a few storks. The elephant trunk has been sawed off, a lifeless limb three feet away. The two front feet have been hacked off. The elephant doesn't have a face. Elena's shutter is clicking and her perfume is mixing in the humid heat with the smell of blood and carcass and I feel faint, terrified of the birds coiling above, circling us like prey.

There are eyes in the trees beyond. I am standing apart from Elena, beside a termite mound. She is looking at me, and then we hear shouts, running footsteps, *Listen to me*, she hisses, *listen. Run.* She is already finished speaking, falling, face forward in a kind of dance, her body falling over in red and white. And then I am picked up, thrown roughly into the tree. Sam enters, yelling, already taking his shirt off to wrap Elena until the distinctive shot that claps Sam's hand to his own chest, his head falling back to the sky. He let himself go, in that moment, and then Elena is being dragged away, her hand trailing through the dust. And I am nowhere, because there is nothing there, nothing to hold on to except the green leaves raining like water dripping, the animals howling below me, and I above them, ready to pounce, to break their brightness with my own, except that I can't move.

I've spent a lot of time wondering what Sam knew when he showed up at Forester's house that morning, talking about how his ring meant something. I think he must have known he would die the next morning. Even though Sam was bitter and angry about the world and the way things were happening, he had a good sense of humor, and would have gone into that mess even knowing what would happen to him. Or maybe he thought he could save her, he must have thought so, the way he ran around yelling at people about what to do, the way he pumped her chest and mopped up blood and tied his shirt around her.

I suppose they are so busy getting Sam and Elena out that I am forgotten, not to mention invisible up in the tree.

I know that for the hyenas, the elephant isn't enough. They want Sam and Elena also. For one instant the elephant trunk which was left lying there is pulled taut, and then devoured. The blood is flying. I listen for her camera, a sign that she might be down there still. I know they are after her and I know she would like this for a photograph, that she would be willing to lie there clicking away as they tear her apart.

The *Crocuta crocuta* is the largest and boldest species of hyena, with long front legs and a square, defiantly shaped head. They travel in packs, are considered nocturnal but are often seen during the day, and eat mostly carrion, rodents, and young animals. Hyenas are actually more closely related to cats than to dogs, which may explain their odd sounds as they fight to eat, not unlike housecats in the backyard mating. The guttural scream and purring laughter are a warning for me but a celebration for them, that they are alive for one moment more—to eat, to cry out, to feel the rain of blood on their backs.

Their celebration is so loud in my ears that I vomit, down through the trees, until the sound is finished, my ears filled with humming blood. The glass sky above glitters and I am dizzy, suffocating, unable to breathe.

When the man finally climbed up the tree, he tried to make me let go of the film. The hyenas were already gone, and the silence had already taken hold. Everything was in place, the place where it would remain from that moment forward.

So that when Jagger decides, for one second, to fall with his voice into some part of himself that can be expressed only with inarticulate sound, surrounded by *I don't know why*, he reminds me of my forgotten knowledge—that the end of the world did happen after all, as I thought, in the image of a man's face. And just as easily my knowledge disappears with the next rift, so that I'm falling backwards into the sound, into oblivion. The reality of my knowledge instantaneously lucid and then instantly gone.

7

When I take my hand from the phone the black plastic is slicked with sweat. I want to call her back, hear her voice again, to make certain she's real. The house has been silent for a while; Forester must be in his room. I am dialing the number, making slow circles with the ancient phone, when I hear shuffling, feet on the porch outside. I don't want to see anyone, especially not Veranu, and I walk quickly down the hall toward the mirror that I hate, the mirror at the end of the world. It holds the image of me in her tight gold dress, dried blood on my neck, my arms and face slashed with dirt and battle. I look away. The mirror is not active; it is not trying to pull me in.

I walk into the guest bedroom, check the closets, try to lock the door that won't lock, and sit down and look through some magazines. Once I'm sitting I can't move, and then I am gone, asleep.

I wake to the sun shining off the rose-colored walls, the light hot pink. The dress is roped around my waist. I disentangle myself and throw it to the ground and lie there, the air tingling my skin.

I listen to the sounds of the house, mostly muffled, like silverware clinking and voices talking, Mira running, *pat pat pat pat,* she seems to run everywhere she goes; various footsteps here and there, music on and then off again; an engine outside, tires on the gravel, a car door slams.

It must be late in the afternoon. It's hot.

There is a new resonance to the voices now, more inflection for the new arrival, more bustling about.

I get up and put the dress back on, not thinking about it, and am on my way to the bathroom to wash my face, when I hear Elena's voice. In the hallway, her voice, something about how she would love some tea.

I forget about my face and walk down the hall.

When someone is dead their identity and your understanding of them is fixed, or it can be. Since they do not change, you do not have to alter your comprehension of their subtly changing being if you do not want to.

But there she is in the living room. I feel a gnawing anxiety at her presence, even while feeling the relief that she is here, alive. She is oddly dressed in a kind of casual business-type suit, matching skirt and jacket and high-heeled clogs with bare legs.

She peers at me, "My god what happened to you?" She walks toward me so that I have to back away. "Where did you get that dress? And your face—"

I can't believe she is here, invading this space.

"I'll take a shower," I say, and then turn around and lock myself in the bathroom.

I can hear Forester ask, "So what are you doing with yourself, Elena?"

I take a shower and afterwards, looking in the mirror at my pale emotionless eyes, it occurs to me: it was not Elena who died in Africa in 1975 when I was nine—it was me. She is in the living room, talking to Forester. Alive and threatening.

I pull on jeans and a tank top and walk slowly down the hall. I can hear their voices.

They are sitting down, Forester on the zebra skin couch, Elena in a chair diagonal from him. She is already laughing that low laugh, already pronouncing her words differently, each letter enunciated, formalized, like she's suddenly from Britain.

Forester has his legs stretched out, his face extra-animated, his moody haziness a little different, something he comes in and out of, as though distracted. And he is suddenly British too, though more subtly, a little spin on each word.

For a while I see only a series of gestures, of looks, her leg crossing and uncrossing, their words filled with a secret communication from the past.

And then I can hear him saying, "Come on, let me see it."

She swings her jacket aside and lifts her top a little.

The bullet went into her back and out through her side, so that there are two scars, and she turns so that he can see them both at once, her side to him, her shoulder lifted. A few lines of stitching snake around the indentations. I've only seen her scars once before, accidentally. The one time I asked she said no.

"Impressive, wonderful. How do you like them?" Forester asks.

"I don't," she says.

"You should. I got one since you were last here." He stands up and pulls down his jeans. He's wearing boxer shorts with faded hearts on them.

"Look here." He points to a chunk of flesh missing from the back of his thigh. "Rhino. Almost as good as yours."

Veda is walking in and out, and I am standing at the entrance to the living room, but Forester and Elena seem oblivious, their eyes on each other, never deviating.

"I was going to go back to him," she says, rudely, I think, and out of context.

But he takes it in stride. "Of course you were. But we had something too."

"There is a kind of . . . *blindness,*" Elena says, her voice low but directed at Forester like a laser, "which is more sinister than deliberate harm—an arrogance that sees only what one wants to see. For a while, when I had something to prove, I was like that—I *wanted*—that's it—I just wanted. It didn't matter what. And so I was like you. You want everything you see, anything you can imagine. You want."

"Like Pac-Man," Forester says.

"What's a Pac-Man?"

"Like a parasite," he says.

"Like someone who is Godless," Elena says. "Like someone who thinks that they *are* God—that everyone and everything is their creation."

Forester grins. "And who's to say?"

There is nothing worse for me than listening to my mother discuss blindness. I walk through the room and out the door, so that I am with Veda on the porch, overlooking the yard.

Mira has a pet pig, a rather hairy hog of some sort, who is quite sweet, and I play with Mira and the hog for a while. It fetches sticks and brings them back, though she drops the stick several feet from me, which gives Mira a chance to find a new one each time.

Later, after a tortuous dinner, after Elena and Forester and Veda enter into a nostalgic discussion of their own, I sit in the library and flip through hundreds of Forester's albums. I realize with shame that I've made a terrible mistake: *Blood on the Tracks* was copyrighted in 1974. The album Dylan recorded the year we were living in Africa, in 1975, is *Desire*. This is why I have never been able to understand Elena, because I was listening to the wrong album. *Desire* is moody, and I crank it up loud, searching for clues. I know I am illogical and absurd, and that I should go to her and talk, face to face. But talking to Elena has always been bizarre for me, and has never worked. It seems easier to find her here, hidden in this music, ready to be discovered.

Except that after two songs Elena steps out the side kitchen door. I'm worried that she will drive away and disappear as suddenly as she appeared, so I get up and follow her out. She is under the bright stars, walking around in the night wind. I sit down on the veranda. Insect candles glow all around the porch, smelling of citronella, strong and faintly unpleasant.

Forester steps out to the porch and stands about five feet away from me. Elena turns around and wanders over. She leans against the veranda to speak to him. "The sky is so big here," she says, her eyes lifting to the stars.

Forester stubs out his cigarette and throws it over the railing.

Elena walks around the porch and out of view. I grab one of the flashlights from a basket by the door and follow her across the creaky boards and down to the yard. She is just standing around back at the edge of the house.

"Come," I say to her.

"What?"

"I want you to see something."

She follows me across the yard and over to the row of Acacia and olive trees. I stop, shining the flashlight on her gravestone.

She breathes in. A sharp inhalation. I have to turn away for a second.

The dirt has been put back over the hole. It is packed hard, but you can see where I dug it up.

She laughs. I feel her laughter like a tickle at the back of my neck, the shiver down my spine, her laughter getting down inside my body, just as Sam used to say.

"I had dreams about this," I say. "About your grave."

Elena stands tall and straight, and I see her for one moment as a solid mass, a breathing woman with a mysterious emotion in her voice.

"You know," she whispers, "I wasn't conscious when Sam died. He saved my life and then died before they even got him to Nairobi. When I saw his body I fainted. His eyes were still open. I'm sure they took their sweet-ass time getting him to the hospital."

I feel a chill imagining Sam. There is an old superstition: if a man dies with his eyes open, he is watching who will follow him.

"Did you really love Sam?" I whisper.

"Of course," she says, her voice loud in the night. "Why do you have to nitpick everything?"

"I just don't understand how you made the choices you—"

"Well, this one was Forester's idea; he thought I'd seen too much. Veranu told him I'd be killed in the hospital if I didn't get out of the country. I had seen face to face, had photographed even, the leader of the largest poaching gang in history. In the news they make it seem like it's stragglers coming in, trying to make a little money for their families. But this whole scene was heavily controlled by a mafia-type organization. I didn't know that until my night in the hospital. Forester came in and told me they would try to kill me even there. So we decided to let them think I had died at the hospital so they would forget about me. I think even Veranu thought I was dead, I don't know. I probably shouldn't be here. When I left, I relocated, sent for you, and forgot it."

"Why didn't you ever tell me anything?"

"It's not important."

"It's important to me. They pretended you were dead. I was nine. I halfway believed them."

"You knew what was going on," she insists. "Forester's driver took me down south on an excruciatingly painful ten-hour ride, to another airport, with my bullet wound still bleeding, and I flew out with a fake passport to Washington, DC with Sam's body."

"How did Forester get you a fake passport?"

"What?" she asks, almost laughing. "That part is easy. Try the rest."

She bends down and runs her hands fully through the dirt, then leans against her name. I kneel down beside her. "Manu's bones are in that coffin. And ivory. I dug it up," I say. "Forester says the ivory is yours. That Veranu gave it to you. As payment for Sam."

"Tell him he can have it back."

"I'm not sure, but I think that would be to disrespect him, as he would say."

Her laughter is a strange, hollow shivering. She is curled up next to the gravestone, her entire side pressed against it.

"If you really loved Sam—" I insist, thinking of Michael, "why did you leave to be with Forester? Why didn't you just know in your heart that Sam would—?"

"Don't ever use that word, *heart*," she interrupts, spitting at the ground. "What the hell is that?"

And then she is weeping, her shoulders shaking, holding onto the stone like she would a lover.

And in my body I feel the release. What we hold in, our children inherit.

Her grief has been in my body long enough. I leave her there, with the flashlight.

Inside the house things are pretty quiet. *Desire* is over, Veda is walking around, speaking in French on the phone.

The house smells like cooked meat. The dinner was some sort of antelope.

I go into my room, sit down, and close my eyes. I know I said all the wrong things to Elena, I know now as well that Forester is wrong—I am ruthless too, but my ruthlessness takes on a strange form. When I found the difference between us somehow irreconcilable, my comprehension of her stopped, my mind fixed on that fault line, and I was able to secretly deny her.

I wake in the middle of the night, my throat dried out completely, and stagger through the darkness and into the kitchen for some water. The moon is shining silver through the living room windows. As I'm returning, walking toward the mirror at the end of the hall, I am seized, frozen with fear. It seems active tonight, and I carefully avoid looking at it. I focus instead on the floor.

The rug is crooked. There is a small crease that shortens the rug near the wall and reveals a thin, narrow lever glinting out between a floorboard and the wall. It's the same kind that was on the coffin. I kneel down and push and turn one end. It unlocks with a cold knife sound, metal against metal. I am afraid I will find all the bodies of the world beneath this mirror.

The lid squeaks as I lift it, revealing a hole in the floor, about twice as wide as my body. I close it gently and get up to find a flashlight. They are kept out on the back porch, and I'm irrationally afraid to go out there, so instead I return with a candle and matches from the kitchen. I lean down into the dark hole. The dirt sides are held up with some kind of clay mortar and a series of two-by-fours. There is nothing immediately visible. I hesitate to step down in, knowing that anything could be under there, and whatever it is is not my business. I lay on the dirty rug that lines the hallway and hold the candle down as low as I can, but I can't see anything else, so I get up and step down into the hole. The air is cool and damp, and I hold the candle out, and there lies a tusk, just out of view from the entrance, as long as my body. The tip is toward me, the surface marred with dirt, incisions, scrapes, just like the one in the coffin. For one fleeting moment I feel a kind of thrill, like an archeologist might when finding something that no one has seen before, something ancient, something hidden.

I place my hand on the tusk, and it seems a cold living thing, a breathing porous life.

The pit I am in appears to be not just a hole but a tunnel. I scoot along the length of the tusk, clamping my hand around the matches, illuminating my way with the candle, which flickers a little in the draft.

At the base of the tusk there is another one, shorter, a little thicker, a faintly flushed pink color. I remember talk about rose ivory: more delicious to behold when carved, glowing pink like rainbow quartz or a flying flamingo. For some reason the tusk overwhelms me with sadness. My throat fills with liquid and I spit, watery like when you're going to throw up. I skim the lighted candle across the surface of the tusk, looking for any luminous flesh of tusk beneath the dirt and scratches. A living thing trapped, hidden, buried, silenced. My throat is sore and swollen and my hands are cold, as cold as the ivory.

Under my hand the tusk becomes a body and I cry; I'm weeping before I even know it. I feel as though I have found a body, buried here, hidden, secret. And I feel that I will never go back, will never get to any place in myself that is alive. And then I am sobbing, thinking about Michael and all the time I've wasted, about his body, some day to be buried like this, and my own.

I'm deep in this emotion when I'm jolted into fear by the sound of footsteps. I have to get out. I crawl quickly toward the entrance and freeze. I feel a vague silent presence, like when the television is on with no sound. I feel prickly and begin to sweat. Then I crawl quickly over to the door and look up, and in the mirror hanging at the end of the hall, just above me, is her image, Elena, just standing there, as though out of nowhere. I see only a glimpse, like she's a ghost, and then the trap door closes quickly, without warning, the bolts scraping securely across each other. Her image is what makes me scream, without even wanting to I'm screaming as loudly as I can, a long high-pitched wail that won't end.

Even as Forester lifts the trap door, even as he reaches his hand down to mine, a crouching shadow over my head, even as he hisses,

"Stop it, it's all right," the scream does not stop. I would like to stop it, but I can't.

He jumps down beside me, clamps his hand over my mouth, his fingers tasting sweet like dope.

"I'm sorry," I whisper, "I couldn't stop."

Forester speaks soft, his breath in my ear, "You should have screamed like that the other night."

This almost makes me laugh, but her reflection is still there. I am up to my waist in the trap and she appears very tall, standing like she's balancing a book on her head, very straight. Forester jumps out, pulls me up. The mirror image seems to waver.

Elena speaks, "I don't think you should be . . ." Her voice trails off.

I feel the hard edges of Forester's body. He fixes the trap door and the bolt and the rug. He takes a pack of cigarettes out of his shirt pocket and stands there, lighting up. Elena is looking at me with disapproval, almost disgust. Her body is tense, and I know she wants me to apologize, somehow redeem myself. She is visibly sucking the breath out of my body. I will soon be an empty shell. She is taking my life.

I take refuge, as I step to the side, in Forester's smoke, which is iridescent, mobile, volatile, blue, and I breathe it in, making time with his breath. Forester doesn't seem to actually care about a whole lot, and I lock onto him with ease, even in his anger, even in his crudeness, and I feel light. Elena is trying to pin me to this spot, and her perfume is making me dizzy, and I am fine again until Forester moves away from me, down the hallway, toward her, around her, and on into the living room.

Sadness overcomes me as he moves away, for it's over now, between us. Elena is standing in his place, boring her eyes into me.

"I'm sorry about Sam," I think to say, trying to find some ground to share.

She looks at me steadily, "Not your fault," she says. "And you should be apologizing to someone else."

I actually believe that Sam's death is partially my fault, but to explain the long trajectory of this to her would be impossible and makes me realize that the suffering I've done for her sake has been meaningless. It did not reach her, and it was not my suffering.

"What was it like to get shot?" I ask her.

"That was a long time ago," she says, already wandering down the hallway.

I feel a bizarre rage fill my entire body. She is willing to share it with Forester, but she is closed off to me.

"Don't you ever wonder who shot you?" I say.

She turns around and walks back until she is facing me. She speaks quietly, with a timbre to her voice. "There is something you don't understand about me. I don't waste time on regret. I don't waste time wondering why—or if it was my fault, like you do. You could blame yourself for anything that took place. If it was my fault? So what? I'll do better next time. I can't go back. You're looking for mystery where there isn't any. It just *is*. It's just *this*." She waves her arms as though at the walls.

"Don't you think you could try harder?" I say.

She looks at me and is about to walk away like she always does, and then she changes her mind. She takes a deep breath. "That makes no sense to me. I don't go inside of something and tear it apart trying to understand every detail."

"Why not?"

"Because it's *past*," she says.

The rage is still there, an intense fire in the pit of my stomach rising up to my arms.

"It's not past. It's defining *now*," I say.

It makes me think she's not alive. I have a desire to attack, throw myself on her back, rip her apart.

We stand there in the hallway for a moment. "Good night," she says.

I lean against the wall and the spikes return. There is one emerging from the wall behind me, sliding into my throat.

She moves away, following Forester. I can't move and my eyes are stinging. But after a few minutes I can hear their voices in the kitchen, in a kind of argument. It occurs to me finally to wonder why they are awake at this hour. I walk down the hallway in the trail of Elena's perfume, and as I walk the spike slices down so that it cuts through my heart, causing searing pain as I breathe.

They are in the kitchen, in crisp silhouette. There is one small light on behind Elena. She is sitting Indian style on the kitchen counter and wearing silky blue pajamas. Forester is leaning against the sink and talking, heaviness in his voice.

"There are some worlds," he says, "when you enter them you never come out. They define you or alter you even against what you might want, and to try to extricate yourself only makes you more entangled, like an insect in a web, the more you tug the more you are entrapped. It's as simple as you tugging—you tug, it alters the entire universe, and now you're responsible for the whole goddamn mess."

When I step in, Elena's voice echoes out of nowhere.

"Get out," she says.

Forester looks at me. He is drinking what looks like a glass of water. He hasn't shaved since I arrived, and his face is rough with brown and white whiskers. The kitchen clock says 3:10.

"It's all right," he says, placing his hand briefly on Elena's knee, shifting his weight. "Let her stay. I can tell you both something."

He reaches backwards to the drawer behind him and takes out a plastic bag of pot. There are a few joints already rolled up, and he takes one out, lights it with some matches from above the sink.

Out from the silence, the strike and swell of the match, his inhalation, the crackling paper, and nothing else.

"Tell us what?" I finally ask.

"Veranu claims that he shot Sam," he says slowly, "but I think he's just trying to protect me. I was shooting at someone across the clearing; I was low in the grass. I never forgave myself that stupid shot. The last time I made a mistake shooting I was fifteen. When I shot him—that was the first time I realized I was fallible. Really. Before then, I was God."

I'm not stoned but I can feel each molecule of Forester's joint burning. I think, each joint, each kitchen, each individual, each sink even, is unique, because each combination of molecules is unique. The metal in that sink is nowhere else. It's here and nowhere else. Each molecule is its own self. You can have *fifty* sinks, all in a row, all identical, and they're not identical at all; each one is unique. Each one with its own molecular structure that has an infinite number of variations. And that's just a sink. Think of elephants, or people, or worlds. Forester flicks his ash into the sink, his paper scintillating, his voice, his words, already gone, in the air, nowhere. A moment already passed, already lost.

"And, you know, there's more to tell," Forester says. "Like Veranu's son, Manu, shot Elena on purpose, so no one else in his group would." He turns to her. "You probably didn't know that?"

She shakes her head.

"Manu was always a better shot than I was. It pissed me off. He was amazing, that boy. And Veranu saved your life," he points at me, "by throwing you into that tree. Risked his life, really, acting as a traitor."

Elena is looking down now. Staring at her ankles. Forester quietly stabs out his joint in the sink, a small sizzling sound.

I wonder if Elena is ashamed. I want desperately to speak, to stop the silence that is breaking out like a wave over the kitchen.

But Forester pushes himself away from the counter, shuffling his feet as he walks out of the kitchen, not looking at her, not looking at me.

8

I am in a deep sleep when her perfume enters my room, inhabits it like a ghost, until I feel her breath on my skin, shaking my shoulder, waking me up.

"I'm on my way to the site," she says. "Forester said you wanted to see it. Let's go. It's best in the morning, like it was then. We'll probably see some elephants."

Her presence next to me feels like a live wire. It's somehow out of character for her to care about such a thing.

"It's past, just leave it alone," I remind her.

"Come on. You can't come to Africa and not see the elephants. Wake up."

She shakes my shoulder again.

With most people I have felt somehow slippery, like I can always escape them, but I feel atoms colliding like I felt last night, how someone standing next to you can alter the alignment of your molecules, as though my cells themselves are somehow vulnerable, because with Elena I have not been so slippery; I have not been able to see where or how she inflicts her damage.

"Come on," she says, "let's go. I'll meet you at my car in five minutes."

I turn over and sink down into the uncomfortable couch bed.

"I don't need to see it," I say, surprising myself.

She stands there for a few seconds, waiting. I remain silent.

"Okay, ten minutes then. I'm leaving in ten minutes."

I turn over and fall back to sleep.

When I wake, the house is unusually quiet. I look around and find everyone outside, Forester pacing the driveway, talking on the phone, and Veda holding a phone as well, their other line. When it rings she answers immediately, speaking in Swahili. Mira is building a rock pile under the porch. She likes the rocks with stripes.

Elena's rental car is gone.

The air is an even, pale yellow, warm and breezy. It's about four in the afternoon.

Veda pauses for a moment in her speech and then resumes.

I look out at the backyard. I hear music from everywhere at once: shifting in the wind through my hair, pulsing through the giraffes on the plain, in the cadence of Veda's speech, the same cadence as a walking impala. Her voice is so insistent, so hesitant at the same time, so much like a news report, that mechanized speech they use to report events that do not concern you personally but are of public interest.

I have a vague desire to ask Forester about the piano player that night, the one who used to play for him. What music was he playing? And how heavy are the tusks beneath his floor? And who bribed him for what?

But my interest is different today than it was yesterday. I expect nothing. The wind is enough of an answer.

Forester walks toward me, still on the phone, speaking Swahili, and Veda is moving away, into the yard, after Mira who is running to the giraffes on the horizon.

Forester stands before me and holds the phone away from his ear for a second.

"Did Elena go to the airport?" he asks me.

"I don't think so. She went to the site," I say. "Why?"

"Another bomb," he says, and continues talking on the phone.

I feel cold. It was stupid of me to call her. I always want to turn back, redo everything, but is that really more predictable than going forward?

Forester is walking toward me again. His shirt unbuttoned, phone to ear. He's wearing the same clothes he was yesterday.

"Why is she here, anyway?" he asks. "To protect you from me?"

I shrug, "I doubt that. Too late anyway, huh?" I laugh, but he just stands there, grim-faced.

"What kind of bomb?" I ask.

"It blew up an airplane. The airport is in chaos. You can't leave the country. They're searching everything, everyone."

"What kind of airplane?"

"A private job—an ambassador's plane. Parts of the plane are on the other side of the airport. But why did she show up here?" he asks. "And where is she now?"

"Elena's here because I told her Sam was alive," I say.

"You *what?*"

"Well, you said . . . Sam could come to dinner."

Forester drops his grim expression and laughs out loud, his head back, catching his balance on the railing.

"Well, she didn't come back for him," he says. "And she shouldn't be wandering around looking for the so-called site. There's a guerilla war on—doesn't she listen to the news?"

"I'm sure."

"Did she talk to you this morning?"

"She woke me early—I don't know when."

"Well, she was gone by seven, when Veda woke up, so it's been at least—" he looks at his watch, "nine hours."

"Is that a long time? For being out?" I ask.

"Yeah—and no. But she shouldn't be at that site. There's a war, and she's trespassing."

"Well, I can't control her," I shrug, "and I doubt she cares. She wanted to see the elephants."

"Damn it," Forester raises his voice at me. He's angry. "You two are screwing up my life. It's distracting. I was about to sell this place. I can't live here anymore."

"What are you talking about?" I ask. "I'm not trying to dissuade you from selling it."

"If you were to come out of yourself and stand *here*. Right here," he points down at the boards that make up the veranda, "and just listen to me," he says, but I realize he's not really talking to me. He's looking out at the hills. "I mean, I can't keep fighting this place."

I don't want to be standing on the porch, on the creaky boards that are worn smooth, smelling Forester's coffee breath and thinking about where Elena is. I'm freezing. I want to put on jeans and a sweatshirt and make a call. I want to call Michael.

Listen to me, Forester just said. Didn't Elena say that too? *Listen to me. Run.*

A breath can take you down to hell.

It so happens that ivory is a perfect density for piano keys, porous enough so that the player's fingers don't stick to the keys but don't slide off either. Between 1860 and 1930, pianos became increasingly fashionable, and the general population became wealthy enough to buy a piano for their sitting room. Between 1860 and 1930, 100,000 elephants were killed annually to provide piano keys in Europe and the United States, and while they also manufactured billiard balls, business cards, domino pieces, snuff boxes, and barrettes, it takes a pound and a half of ivory for every keyboard, and by 1910, 350,000 pianos were made yearly. For every pound of ivory, one man, woman, or child died en route, carrying the ivory from central Africa to the coast. The slaves were routinely starved, tortured, and raped, and at the coast, sold along with the ivory.

Approximately those same years in North America, in the late 1800s, the sixty million bison that roamed the prairies were shot by Europeans for either their tongues, considered a delicacy, or for sport, often from moving trains. By 1900, bison were extinct east of the Mississippi River, and there were only two wild herds left in the northwest, one near Yellowstone Park and another in Canada. This in some ways explains the rush for elephants—ivory was only part of it—the men with guns were out of bison.

On the surface all of this means nothing—a choice between elephants and Beethoven, between slavery and commerce, between wildness and culture. But the choice has already taken place.

Forester chose Elena. Or she chose him, I don't know. She added to her photographic collection of data and evidence: culled and poached elephants, piles of ivory waiting to be sold, elephants that starved in the drought.

I walk around the driveway, staying warm in the sun, looking for some good rocks for Mira's collection. She looks at my most recent rock, one white stripe through gray. She takes it, licks it to better show the stripe.

Forester walks by.

"Can I use your phone for a second?" I ask.

He hands it over. I run inside, find my address book, and dial Trey's number. The phone rings as I walk through the house, and rings as I walk down the driveway and is still ringing when I hang up. I call Michael's number in Albuquerque. His message machine answers and I tell him that I can still remember the exact sound of his backward-beating heart, and that time must work like this: ten years can seem like ten minutes.

After I hang up I think that I could have told him what day it is, or that I can see the outline of giraffes as the sun lowers itself, slowly, steadily, into the horizon. But Forester is on the other side of his car and is motioning that he wants the phone back.

"Can we go looking for Elena?" I ask him, as he takes the phone.

But he's pushing buttons, walking in a tight circle.

In 1915, just around the time that Isak Dinesen made the Ngong Hills in Kenya her home, a tusk could weigh as much as 235 pounds. Today the average tusk weighs 22 pounds, which is the tusk of a twelve-year-old male elephant, and because their life cycles are identical to ours, it's the equivalent of killing a twelve-year-old boy because there are no older males left alive.

In the 1980s, 70 percent of the world ivory was imported into Japan and 70 percent of that was used to make *hanko*, a seal of identity (like a rubber stamp, functioning in society like a fancy business card) for individuals. In the early 1980s when the Japanese got rich, it was a fashionable sign of wealth and prestige to have a very nice *hanko,* and since everyone had money, there were two million Japanese walking around with ivory *hanko.* Ivory happens to be just porous enough to soak up and put out the ink perfectly.

At the same time the Japanese all got rich, the arms import in Africa increased from 500 million in 1971 to 4,500 million in 1980. As soon as the civil wars and wars of liberation got a little chaotic, as wars can do, the weapons found their way into countless hands that wanted power and wealth, and one way to get that in Africa was to hunt for ivory.

I didn't know that we were there for the same thing as everyone else. I thought we were there to help. But we were there for what we could get, and when Elena got Forester, she thought she was getting the world.

When Forester uncoils his pace he hands me back the phone.

"I guess I don't need it," I say.

He places his hand on my head for a second, and then it falls to my shoulder. He starts talking, right in the driveway, about how a gardener of his was beaten to death with a rock one night while he slept. He tells me that one summer night Veda's father was out taking a walk when a car gang armed with AK-47s ran him down, shot him for sport. He tells me that there is a suburb called Karen, after Karen Blixen. Instead of hills and wind there are locked gates, guard dogs, a regular street where Dennis, Karen's lover, used to land his plane. He tells me it's like going from having sex with someone you love, to looking at cheap porn magazines. He tells me that the Kikuyus he used to know are now rich and dress primarily in Armani and live in guarded country homes. He says it is bizarre and surreal and heartbreaking. And gesturing all around us, toward the dead tree down his driveway, his voice cracking, he says, you can't think about it, but he swears to God, this was paradise. Every tree was a tree of life, a tree of heaven, with hundreds of animals everywhere. You never looked for an elephant. They were just there. And then, after a pause, he recovers, his voice no longer low as he throws the burning ember of his cigarette to my feet. I stamp it out.

"We'll look for Elena tomorrow," he says. "If she's in trouble, I doubt we can find her, and if not, she'll be back. We can't go at night."

I think about how when I first saw Forester in front of those hills, I saw sex, seduction, power. But I was mistaken, just like Sam. I didn't see sex at all. I saw death.

As soon as Forester leaves my side, I feel it all happening at once. There is no clear order. *Now* is she dead? Because if she is, it is my fault for sure. And it is not something I wanted, not even something I anticipated. I feel a million black spiders emerge from their eggs in my stomach. They crawl around, up my throat, growing rapidly as they destroy the inside of my body, eating away at my flesh. All my organs collapse in a bloody mess.

When it is dark outside Veda serves coconut milk and coffee and fried bananas and evening pancakes, she calls them, small little stacks. The porch lights are pale like the moon. I drink black coffee, trying to kill the spiders.

I must have misunderstood everything. It is silly to imagine that there was a choice between pianos or elephants, to imagine that this moment could be taken out of the context of Hannibal going into Africa, or the English building the railroads, or the direction the first nomadic tribes moved in, or the burst of light to begin with, light that has no mass when it travels but has mass only when it stops, an unquenchable ball of rolling consequences.

Nowadays they don't cull elephants with three Land Rovers and a few guns. They look for a herd of at least fifty or more and take up three airplanes, skimming the air just above the elephants. They shoot the stragglers on the outside of the herd first, from about five to ten yards away using .458 or .308 semiautomatics. When the shooters are good, they can down 100 elephants in less than a minute. They shoot them in the brain, if they can get the shot, or in the spine if the elephant is running away.

When they cull elephants with planes, they kill every elephant in the vicinity and take away all the meat, bones, stomachs, everything. And still—elephants come from every direction to investigate the site. How do they know where it happened? They heard it, through infrasound. They visit, pay respects, then the area is abandoned—no elephant will go near the area, sometimes for several years.

I remember Elena looking at her gravestone. Breathing. Inhaling. Exhaling. Laughing. A breath can take you up to God. Maybe she was not as removed as she seemed, but simply wordless.

When Elena tramped alone through a wooded area with a nine year old trailing, saying, there's a photo up ahead, she was hoping for something more. She wanted to fit into a world she knew nothing about. She knew what nurses know; she knew about illness and injury and how to put something together again. She did not know that most people do not like illness and injury and do not know how to put things together again, but rather how to ignore what they see, which is something I am good at. I never once saw the leprosy and sewage running down the streets, the animals with their heads cut off and the starving septic children. I saw the sun fill up the sky and the elephants fully submerge themselves in water and breathe through their trunks. I saw them wave to one another, their trunks like ribbons, like voices calling across the sky.

The night lasts forever. It is dark and cold and I fall asleep on the porch, and Veda wakes me up and tells me to go inside. I don't. I just sit there, until finally someone brings me a blanket and the citronella candles blow out and there is the moon and the cold bright stars and the strange noises of the night, and I feel the darkness creeping into me and I think, this is good, to be cold and dead and buried on a porch, unmoving and unable to move, tusklike, knowing that I will no longer worry about dying because that is not my business. And then I am carried, half afraid of what Forester is after, but he just tumbles me into the bed, cold, so cold I can't breathe, and then I am alone.

She told me she wished she had never been with my father. That they were no good together. That it's too bad I didn't have another father, too bad, in other words, that I had ever been born. Strange that a human being can come from an accident, not willed, unwanted, but shining before you, demanding sustenance and love. Demanding life itself.

9

I wake up in the guest room, the sun shining through the trees and onto the pink walls so that it looks like pink flowers are blooming all over the room. I creep through the silent house and into a hot shower, the water so hot that I feel like I might collapse, so I lie down in the shower for a while, a hot waterfall. Elena has been missing for twenty-eight hours. Perhaps she is tracking something. I could have told her what I know. I could have told her a few facts about the way in which things can and cannot disappear. Or the way in which people like for those they love to die only once, never more than once.

I decide to dress in my old driving clothes, the polka-dotted bikini top, shorts, and sandals. I feel like driving. I need a car. I could probably find her. I wander out into the sun where Forester is pacing again, talking on the phone, as though in a repeat of yesterday.

As he passes, the sweet smell of weed, and he tosses me a joint, "Light up, you half froze to death last night," he says.

"I'm still here," I mutter, catching the thin cigarette as I fall into my favorite padded porch chair. The cushions are cold.

He stands still for a second, holding the phone away from his ear. "So is your mother. She'll be driving in soon."

I sit up. "You heard from her?"

"Yeah. She saw the guerillas and hid out. Found a ranger and called here. She's all right."

He shakes his head in what might be either disbelief or admiration, I can't tell, and continues talking on the phone.

I hold my hand out and feel the warm breeze. It runs along my face, my legs, my arms. I try to decide if Elena's return means that I'm not alone anymore or if I'm alone again.

I push the neatly rolled joint he gave me into a space between the boards.

There's a whole family of tuskless elephants in Amboseli. The matriarch is tuskless, and she heads a clan of all ages, all tuskless. Even her teenage males, tuskless. They'll never grow tusks. No one knows for sure how this aberration came about. Was their desire to survive so great that they willed their body to act according to their knowledge? A tuskless elephant cannot be shot for its tusks. A scientist would say that an animal cannot *will* genetic change. But to manifest in the body what is present in the mind: for thoughts to become a reality—doesn't that happen all the time?

As Sam predicted, smallpox was visibly eradicated, in an amazing global community effort, on par with the goal of the World Health Organization. For a long time, only two official locations of smallpox existed: the headquarters of Federal Centers for Disease Control and Prevention (CDC) in Atlanta, Georgia, and the State Research Institute of Virology and Biotechnology outside the city of Novosibirsk, in Siberia, Russia, which is a financially troubled former virus weapons development facility.

The smallpox vaccines at the CDC were in aged glass bottles. They were lined up, dusty, yellowed, occasionally crusty. Their potency was in question. Because of evidence of biowarfare laboratories that manufacture smallpox in countries like Iraq, the US government commissioned scientists to extract and purify the smallpox that had been sitting dormant for twenty years. Their job was to stretch the existing supplies and begin reissuing the smallpox vaccine. If smallpox itself wasn't back, the possibility for it was. It is not just Pandora who opens boxes. But we have solutions for such things, vaccination after vaccination. Immunity.

Elena's car approaches a few hours later. In her wake is a low, yellow blizzard of dust. When she steps out, slamming her door, she walks over, happy, apologetic, telling stories of her adventures. Both Veda and Forester are accommodating, standing around, listening, telling their own stories. Elena claims to have seen several young elephants, playing, tripping over one another. No matriarch in sight. When she heard the shooting, she hid out, went back to her car after dark. This morning, on her drive back, she saw black smoke plumes. She heard on the radio about the bomb. But is that smoke from the airport, or something else, she wonders. They ask questions, pointing here and there, ask her more details. She's excited that she can make out some of the Swahili. She needs a camera. Can she borrow one?

I watch her from a distance. I listen only a little. I focus on the faint wind that is dying now, in the heat. I can see the heat. It looks like water falling.

Veda tells the cook to serve appetizers and cold drinks out on the lawn. The cook sets up a round table, brings over chairs, fancy foods, pink tea. Forester is moving two speakers out into the yard as they pound out piano music, I'm not sure what. Veda is laughing at something Elena is saying, and Forester is back to being himself, a smirk on his face and an easy walk. They mill around going here and there, and I pace back and forth on the porch.

And then Elena, en route back from the kitchen after getting an expensive bottle of wine for Veda, stops me on the veranda.

"I'm going to stay here for a little while," she says.

"What? What about your job? Besides, Forester is selling this place."

"Maybe I'll change careers. Or be a nurse in town. Maybe I can help Forester keep the land."

"He doesn't want it."

"He does want it. I need you to take my coffin back for me, though. Can you?"

"Back where?"

"Back home," she says, walking forward a little so that I'm backing up into the doorway. "I'd like to have it," she continues, "There's no point in just wasting Veranu's gift."

"You said you would burn it. You should burn it. What are you going to do with it?"

"I *need* it. To honor Veranu," she insists. She is holding the wine bottle by the neck, swinging it in a short motion, back and forth. Her eyes are steely. "Can you do that?"

I sigh. She's not thinking clearly. "Mom," I say, "I've touched it. I've looked at it. It contains everything evil: greed, money, waste, suffering. Just give it back."

"I can't give it back. Forester doesn't want it and he doesn't want to sell it."

She is blocking the doorway. What makes her think I'm going back? There is something chemical that happens to me when she is active like this. I shut down. As she gains her life, I lose mine.

"Yes, okay, I'll do it," I say, so that she'll move out of the doorway and leave me alone.

"Thank you. You should have come and seen the elephants. The impala."

Forester zooms by, up the steps, into the house. Elena walks out to the yard.

I walk slowly inside. I know what to do next. Forester is changing the music.

"I need to get out of here," I say.

"You can't leave," he says. "You haven't seen anything yet."

"I've seen plenty," I say. "Are the planes leaving Nairobi today?"

Forester looks at me; he is now playing Beethoven.

"I want to get back to my life," I say.

"So what is your life?" he asks, his eyebrows arched.

I ignore that. "This is my question, Forester. Are the planes flying out? Are the buses running?"

"Planes. I believe so. Buses. Never. Never get on a bus in this country."

The music is so loud in the house that I just point to his phone. He hands it over.

I dial Trey's number and no one answers. I try to push down the wave of panic I feel. I carry the phone to my room and start gathering my stuff. I never really unpacked, so it doesn't take long. I roll up the gold dress into my bag and take down Elena's photos from the wall. Some of them are supposedly the last she took, from the roll of film I kept in my hand while I was in the tree. I place them in a zippered pouch in my bag.

I'm thinking, how strange that the two poles don't always line up. How strange that Michael got me to her but that she will not get me back to Michael.

I'm choking and crying like there was some real problem in my life. My chest is caving in with despair. I feel stupid and angry and ashamed. Africa was supposed to solve everything. Everything was supposed to end here.

I dial Trey's number again, but again no one answers.

I take the gold dress out of my bag and have no place to put it. There are no free hangers in the closet. Finally, I fold it into a ball and push it under the pillow.

I unzip the inner pouch and take out the photos of the massacred elephants from my duffel bag. I toss them into the drawer of the bedside table. They slide away from each other, revealing parts of people. There is a man standing, his hair in his eyes, his shirt untucked, looking like he has seen the end of the world. It is a photograph of Michael. There are many birds behind him, in the trees, heavy and dark. The birds look like bodies falling from the sky. I pick up the photo. It is a man leaning on a rifle, a friend of Forester's maybe, not Michael.

I throw the photograph on top of the others and shut the drawer. All my clothes are packed. I look under the bed. I walk out of the guest room and down the hall. I exit the front door and step out to the driveway, where the heat is falling in sheets. The dead tree in Forester's yard looks like a mirage in the distance.

Then I'm walking into it, ready to disappear, ready to be just an apparition on the road. The whole driveway is a streak of light. The dead tree is etched against the sky like a petroglyph. It seems just as magnificent now as it ever was alive, brown, expansive, a hand opening to the sky. And steady on a branch, a large dust-colored bird. It looks like a red-tailed hawk, but of course it isn't. It is probably just a little bigger than Magali. The heat warms my back and blurs my vision, and I can feel my shoulder blades open like wings, as the bird flies away, an outline disappearing. Then I circle back, riding a thermal. I do not flap my wings; I just glide. I look down from above, circling in the hot wind, looking for prey, and it all seems easy, it all seems right, the carnage, the blood, the lack of connection—this is it, the way we love. And then I am on the road again, the barbed wire beside me, and I search for the feeling I always have—the feeling that my mother is about to die—and it seems to be far away, over there, in the falling light.

I'm almost halfway to the highway and when I look back the sun is floating like a rivulet of water through the dead tree. The duffel bag is heavy. Everything is bright. The rocks are bumpy under my shoes. The barbed wire fence is rusted, slack, much of it grown over with tall grass and weeds. I never noticed this before. The road before me, the smoother dirt part, is shining like a mirage; it looks like a long mirror in the heat and my feet are shattering the light as I walk.

10

I'm about half a mile down the driveway when I walk into the ditch and lean down and step through the barbed wire. I walk for a long time, straight out west through the tangled weeds and grass. After a while I stop and just stand there, because it seems to me that this is what I had wanted, to be standing still on the vast moving continent of Africa, feeling the hot wind on my face, the way it whips here, there, in a kind of mystery, like colored scarves at the end of a circling arm, no explanation for such shifts, no explanation for me being buried like Forester's tusks, holding back.

I trample the yellow grass at my feet, and I see why Forester is always looking to the hills in the west; they change colors every few hours, from blue to gray to yellow. And they seem to move as well, to rise up and fall lower in the sky.

When I start walking again I circle around, so that I'll come up on Forester's property as though from the hills. I look back to where I was, and the sun is low in the sky and so bright it looks like it's raining light at the flat edge of the earth.

I see them from a distance, Elena and Veda and Forester all sitting around the small round table in the yard. The table is a spot of blue. Their bodies seem animated, moving this way and that, one arm up, one leg out, another bent. As I get closer they become more solid, Veda taking her wavy brown hair back with her hands, away from her face. Elena standing to demonstrate what she is talking about, her long arms in the end reaching for her iced pink drink. Forester laughing with his head thrown back, like he does. They eat the suspicious-looking breaded finger foods, listen to their music, and plan their future.

When I finally asked Forester, he told me that the music across the plain that long ago morning was a Beethoven sonata. He played, that piano player, all night, lots of nights, on a cocaine high, his fingers dancing on the ivory keys. That piano player, Forester said, played music in a way that could keep anyone alive forever.

As I bend under the fence and walk onto the lawn, I see Mira rise up from the grass, through the gold falling light, singing, *da da da.*

There is a strange feeling of longing that I have always had, always a desire to be someplace better than where I am. But the world I want to enter is always disappearing before I get there, and the world I enter is never the same as the one I dreamed about.

Elena raises her glass at me, do I want some?

Mira runs up to me. She pushes into my hand a flower that looks pretty much like a dandelion. I take it, smiling, at which point she quickly takes a rock from her pocket and holds it out. Then she pulls her hand back, licks the rock, to better show the stripes, and drops it into my palm. It is quite a rock, heavy, encircled with stripes. It seems to spin as I look at it. Someone told me once that they had never met anyone with less faith than me. I didn't understand this. But it seems rather clear right now. The rock is a small spinning spiral. A small resolution. And in the end, all the small resolutions must link together.

And I think that whatever it was I thought about memory I've changed my mind. With memory, you are in time. Without memory you have no time, and to escape from memory is not to access the eternal, like I thought, but to lose it altogether.

I turn back for a second, to look at the large fire that is reaching the sky, and the pink and blue land flattening out beyond that. With the light this low it looks like everyone is on fire. There is a rim of gold and my hands become caught in it. It is evening but it looks like a shining dawn. And then, as I watch, the sun eases down behind the blue hills until it is a glow, a trace on the horizon. I had wanted more and more and now nothing. I kneel down and hand the rock back to her.

"It's beautiful," I say.

And she smiles at me, a smile that really takes me away, open and curved, her eyes disappearing.

11

I didn't leave that night like I thought I would, and the days unfolded quickly. Elena meets some wildlife biologists and immerses herself in an aspect of what she had wanted to do so many years ago: she trains for and becomes an elephant nurse. She stays five days a week at an elephant orphanage about forty miles from Forester's place. With her gone, I have space to breathe, and I stay on, traveling with Forester, taking care of Mira, slowly making friends with Veda. They assure me I'm not a burden, and I do what I can to help them out.

Forester takes me back to the clearing above Cloud Falls twice, and it never has quite the effect I'm looking for, which would be some kind of recognition and comprehension. The drive there is stressful enough, with ominous-looking armed guards at the first two gates we pass. Minutes later Forester weaves off-road through and across a series of barely visible roads until we finally grind our way over bumps and open grass to park near the river.

The hike in takes about thirty minutes, and the landscape changes as we go. It is a strange place, a little difficult to navigate, with dry trees and rough grassy clearings between them. Cloud Falls is about a quarter of a mile from a deep curve in the river.

Forester is a different person once we enter the woods, feral, high-strung, hyper-aware, listening always for poachers and animals, with us stepping on rocks whenever possible, in the river for a moment and then out. We are never on regular park land, it is always illegal, what we are doing, but the only way to Cloud Falls, Forester explains, and he follows tracks for a time, and veers off away from them as well. During our walks he tells me enough horror stories about elephants and their physical and psychological torture, and everything else that is corrupt, to send me into a tailspin. I never know what to do with the information, and I never figure out exactly what Forester does with it.

The second time we visit, we have to quickly climb a tree together to avoid a male elephant on a rampage; he has been shot several times, and puss and blood oozes from the holes in his face and side. His trumpeting is choked and bizarre, and he tears apart anything in his path. His suffering is intense, and I can't watch.

We sit up in that tree for at least an hour, Forester cursing the shooters and saying he should shoot the elephant himself, but there are no good shots from the tree and he isn't in the mood for tracking around an angry elephant to get a perfect shot.

Through Forester's binoculars, I can see white maggots near the elephant's vast and wrinkled ear, a rip and some blood in the same ear, and several long wispy hairs on its trunk. For a while the elephant just rubs up against a tree, tilting his head back, lifting his trunk up into the branches. His sounds are terrible; a clawing at the back of his throat, he seems to be getting tired.

"All right, I'll get down and finish him off," Forester says, a grim look on his face. And just as Forester is about to hit the ground, the elephant is groaning again, and in a fit of anger has knocked down a fairly large tree and is stamping it to bits. Forester is beside me again, breathing hard.

"Couple of rangers can do it," he says. "I'm not so young anymore."

After a while the elephant has disappeared and the wind is blowing faintly with the smell of oranges and mangos and metal, sweet and bitter across my arms and face, and in the moment of sweetness I almost panic. The wind is blowing around my ears and I feel like I can't hear as well as I'd like to. There are birds and insects and maybe an engine in the distance or maybe not. The wind seems to be blowing through my body, through the trees, through the long tangled grass blurring under our feet. My body is being shoved at with spikes, with sharp voices, with a wind that carries danger.

"What's that smell?" I ask Forester.

"It always smells like that here."

"Where was she shot?" I ask.

"Right about over there," he says, pointing to a nondescript patch of long gray-green grass.

There must be an infinite number of things that have taken place on that patch of grass.

I start talking to ease off the strange feeling that is filling my body. As I talk, I peel off little parts of the bark of the tree, and flick off ants and spiders that crawl up and down the branches. I tell Forester, for some reason, about how with Michael came the flashbacks, never with anyone but Michael, and how Elena seems implacable and cold and always has.

He shrugs. "You're in a ramp."

"What?"

"In a ramp. You know. Stuck. If you move, you fall, so you don't move."

"Oh."

"Yeah. I could tell that the moment I saw you. You're doing that post-traumatic stress thing for people who can't handle it."

"What is that supposed to mean?"

"It means you deal with it. You get through it. That's what I told you to do when you were a kid. And you did it. You just have to keep doing it."

"I'm not sure that's the best way, Forester," I say.

"It's the only way," he says. "Come on, lets go."

"You smoke weed constantly," I say, loudly, as he leaps down from the tree. "What is it you can't deal with?"

His look is impervious for a minute and then he almost smiles.

"So I'm in a ramp too," he says. "So what?"

A smell like oranges and mangos is still wafting slowly through the trees. My body is shivering.

I'm sitting alone on the porch one evening, drinking lime tea, when Veda brings the phone out to me.

It's Michael. His voice is warm, instantly relaxing. I had forgotten that his voice could do this.

"So what are you doing?" he asks.

"I was just waiting for you to call."

He laughs.

"Damn," he says. "Same here. I've been waiting a while."

"So what are you doing?" I ask.

"I'm out on the fire escape. I'm picking one person and following them with my eyes for as long as I can see them."

I try to imagine that.

"I'm not doing anything as interesting," I say.

And then we talk about how he's planning to drive back to Albuquerque soon and about Africa and Paige and Forester and our talk continues as the moon rises past my line of vision and he tells me to really take my time here. To stay long enough to really know something about it. And I have to argue, of course, that you can take Africa apart and look at every part of it from all different angles and you still don't really know it.

"Well, maybe one molecule of it then," he says. "Maybe you can know that."

I kind of doubt that even the mystery of a molecule can ever be taken from it, but I take my time. I stay for a few nights with Elena at the elephant orphanage, I travel with Forester as he visits rangers and scientists, and I go with Mira and Veda into Nairobi. There are almost always visitors at Forester's ranch, and they all have personal stories, some funny, some factual, some trivial, but always the subject swings back to the corruption that infiltrates every organization, especially CITES (Convention on International Trade in Endangered Species), and the endless slaughter and torture stories, AIDS, the hunger, the devastation.

I think of getting involved, researching and reporting or staying indefinitely, but it feels binding, like if I begin I will never leave, it will never end.

And one day I wake up to the sun hitting the walls in a furious pink glow, and I realize, I want to go home.

12

In the end, I take Elena's coffin with me. We pack the car on a Sunday afternoon and my mother and Forester both drive me to the Nairobi airport. The coffin is wedged in the back, beside me, and Veranu is smiling and waving at us all the way down the driveway. Forester is feeling talkative and tells me as we drive that u.s. Customs is supposed to x-ray everything that enters the country, but that they are often too busy. After all, he says, they are looking, obviously, for contraband such as bombs and drugs, and not dead mothers or ivory. I'm about to question this when Elena interrupts to tell me, in her usual pragmatic manner, that she so appreciates me doing this for her, and that Veranu appreciates it as well, because for him, it is the completion of a cycle, and for her, it is the completion of an unspoken contract, and in the midst of her droning, I decide to really look at the deep African sky for the last time, and to not argue with either of them.

At the airport, Forester quickly secures two men to carry the coffin over to customs. Then he proceeds to discuss details and paperwork in Swahili and English for about twenty minutes. He hands them the original death certificate for Elena Monroe while Elena is standing right there. He also has an affidavit by a funeral director stating the cause of death. He fills out forms and pays for the shipment and customs and asks about ports of entry into the

United States. Then he tells them which port of entry and what time and hauls over the supposedly hermetically sealed coffin and signs more papers. I suspect Forester knows someone at the point of entry, but I don't dare ask.

It is almost dark by the time we are on the square of asphalt watching them load the coffin. The plane is parked out away from the airport, and lines of workers come and go. The coffin and I will ride in the same plane until we arrive in Paris, and then it will take a different plane out, and arrive one hour prior to me in New York.

Forty minutes late, long after dark, they call for boarding.

Elena hugs me, tells me to be careful, and Forester pulls me forward several steps, across the black asphalt toward the plane, and hands me a thick, musty wad of cash, "for your trip," he says, "parking fees and the like," and he kisses me, half on the mouth, so that his whiskers scrape my skin, and with his cigarette breath in my ear, he says, "This is what you do: unbutton your blouse a little, tell them your mother died in Africa in 1975 and you're bringing back her body, and give them one of those smiles, the kind you give me when you don't believe what I'm telling you, and they'll let you through."

I slip the money into my pocket, push him away, wave to Elena, and walk into the darkness, toward the lighted doorway of the plane.

Once we are far above Africa, in the black sky, most everyone draws the shades over their windows, but for as long as I can I press my forehead against the plastic square and watch the black sky unfold and open up as the stars stay steady, edging a little nearer every second.

I change planes still half-asleep, and stay asleep until we land. New York, as usual, is in fast motion, with the straight trajectories of businessmen, the excited chatter of tourists, and the fast but dull responses at the counters. In the brassy rusted noise of it all I feel like I barely move. I saunter from place to place. I'm wearing Forester's idea of good airport attire: tight black pants, a thin silk blouse, and a black jacket. He had me paint my nails and pull my hair back. He gave me an ex-wife's pair of earrings, blue lapis with little diamond stones. She was a wife between the time of Elena and Veda, apparently. I think I look like a strange breed of airline stewardess. When it takes them an hour to come up with the coffin, I'm not even bothered, I just stand around and wait. There is nothing urgent for me here. When I am called into the little glass room I do exactly what Forester said to do: two men hold all the papers, I unbutton my top button, I smile like I don't believe a word they say, and I tell them my mother died in Africa in 1975 and I'm bringing back her body. They nod, gravely, look me over, shuffle the papers, ask me how she died, even though it says how on the papers, and charge me an extra hundred dollars in transaction fees.

Then I am walking the long smooth corridors, faces passing me like clouds. I pull my mother's coffin, tied to the metal rings of the cart behind me, to the bus station for a bus that will take me to long-term parking.

I step out, into bus fumes and clumps of people and a feeling of dirty rain.

"What have you got in here?" the bus driver asks me, while another driver automatically helps him lift and shove it into the lower depths of the bus. The coffin looks worn and scratched, though Forester glossed it up with polyurethane. It's a perfect wooden rectangle, like a long coffee table, or a very long trunk. I don't answer the driver; I just climb on board.

I sit up high, the ride gliding, the twenty or so passengers saying insignificant things, but I'm in wonder that I understand every word they say, unlike in Africa.

Later I walk up to the bus driver and proceed as a stewardess might; I'm chatty and nice. He ends up dropping everyone else off and then winds the bus down the aisles between cars.

Stewardesses don't drive crappy cars, but I have no choice.

"That white car." I point, and he pulls over.

"What have you got in here?" he asks again as he swings up the lower door to the bus.

"It's a coffin. It's my mother," I say.

He takes in a long breath. "Oh. Didn't realize. It's small for a coffin."

"Is it?" I ask.

"Oh yeah. Caskets are huge. You can't carry them."

It's old, I almost say, and was handmade in Africa, but he is scrunching up his eyes as though trying to evaluate the situation and looks confused enough already.

He needs a tip, for driving me down the aisle with the cars. I almost forgot. I turn my back to him casually for a second and peel off a fifty. I hand it to him. He doesn't just slip it in his pocket, he takes his wallet out of his back pocket and places the money carefully in there.

Then he squints at my car. "It might be small for a coffin, but it still won't fit," he says.

"It will," I argue.

He's looking at me now. I realize that's not what a stewardess would say. I bite my lip and lean on my car. I watch a few seagulls that are circling the other side of the parking lot, white birds against a blue-white sky.

I look back at his face, worn and reluctant.

"Well," I say, "it will be a challenge."

"Yes," he sighs.

So together we lift and push and maneuver for about fifteen minutes, wedging the rectangle into the passenger feet area, along the folded-down seat, so that it stretches all the way back. Technically, he is correct, it doesn't fit, and he helps me tie the trunk down using two of my socks.

Then he says good-bye, and I drive to the gate. I peel off eight hundred and ten dollars for seventy-five days of parking, and I still have a big wad of cash. Forester's cash makes me smile, the way it buffers me from everything. I have no idea how much is there and I have no desire to know. I enter the highway and then exit soon after, driving the wasted and splayed streets of Queens looking for a mechanic. I pull in, and for the hour and a half it takes them to change my oil, replace a fan belt, and adjust the tires and brakes, I listen to the piston and hydraulic sounds of the garage.

When I peel off more than two hundred dollars to pay the steely-eyed mechanic, I feel what it must be like to go from having nothing to feed one's children to wearing Armani suits, and for the first time in my life, I feel the power of money instead of the corruption that so often seems to lie beneath it.

I get stuck in New York traffic until late, but she is stretched out beside me, and the smell of Africa is in the wood, and I feel empowered. I drive for sixteen hours, stopping only for gas.

When I arrive in Nashville that night I'm a nervous wreck. The slow wave of Africa that has been in me has died off and I feel a quickening. I want to keep driving, but I can't really focus, so I decide to check into a motel. Some kind of pine air freshener fills the room and makes breathing unpleasant. I lie down on the bed and turn on the TV. I find out about a local scandal, that it's August 23rd, and clear skies are predicted for tomorrow. I decide to take a shower. I touch the cheap shower curtain and cringe; it's slimy. I open up all of the tiny pink and cream-colored bars of soap, and then I can't use them—they all smell like chemicals. I try to wash away from the plastic paneling one dark hair curling across the wall but it won't go away. I finally use the cream-colored bar of soap to dislodge it.

After my shower, I can't sleep because I'm afraid for the coffin, so I dress in my old summer clothes, shorts and a bathing-suit top, and go out and fall asleep in the car. I leave Nashville when all the houses are still dark, just a creeping wedge of light behind me.

By this time I hate interstates; I can't stand the idea of remaining on Interstate 40 for another nineteen hours, so I cut off onto a scenic road. It leads south; I'll find my way back later.

The roads rise and fall and the heat is relentless. Thick greenery crawls over the sign for the railroad tracks. I fill up my gas tank at a dilapidated pink house that has a 7UP sign and gas. Inside, you can buy corn nuts and Southern Comfort. It is slow here, and eyes follow me, so I move slowly, the air wet and suffocating. Verdurous ivy covers all the telephone poles, and a mist lies in the trees. I keep driving, down blue curving roads, past factories and bowling alleys, and then I'm on a street with a white steeple and shops and cafés. There are only a few people on the streets, and the light casts around randomly. I scan the radio stations several times, then finally open my door and follow the warm sidewalks, watching the leaves in the trees shake off their light. I have to shuffle my sandals to maintain contact with the ground; it rolls and falls under my feet as though I'm still driving.

In a shop window, sun glints off a pair of sunglasses. The glasses seem like something I need, and as I enter, cowbells tied together with a rope ring against the door. I pick up the glasses by their leather side covers. They are heavy. I rotate them, and see the steely reflection of the room on the glass. There is a strange sound, like a thousand clocks ticking.

"Those are aviator glasses," a voice speaks from behind me. "Not for sale, just for display," she breaks off, then continues, "given out to pilots in the Vietnam War."

I spin slowly around, into a labyrinth of blown-glass lamps, tiled coffee tables, gilded mirrors, and clocks, hundreds of clocks, ticking.

An old woman stands halfway across the store.

"It's like rain. The sound of all these clocks." I manage to speak. The woman says nothing.

I slip the glasses on, and gold overtakes the edges of everything.

"I have clocks from all over the world," she says, her voice a deep timbre.

I had just reached for the glass door, which I notice is blotted and smeared.

I turn around again. The clocks are ticking; hundreds of them, clicking like water dripping.

"They chime every hour," she says. "I wind them myself. It takes me about eight hours. Wait, so you can hear them. Soon it will be eleven o'clock."

I stand there, starving, wondering about the sound they make and about the glasses.

She leads me around the store. She points to a dark, basic clock on the wall behind her. "This one's an original," she says, "one of the first clocks built for the London train station. It's very precise." She shows me others: porcelain, from France; marble, from Russia; one of the first moving ship clocks from Switzerland; clocks in the shape of arches, horses, boxes, circles; from China, from India, from all over Europe, from the pioneers, for fireplaces; for carrying around.

"What about Africa?" I ask.

"Africa?"

"Clocks from Africa. Do you have any?"

She stands as though stunned for several seconds. Then she becomes upset, looking here and there, muttering. The clocks are ticking.

"It really doesn't matter," I tell her. "I was just wondering."

"This is the thing. I really have nothing from Africa in this store. That is a tragedy. Once, many many years ago, young lady, I had a zebra skin. I sold it for a lot of money, too. That must have been from Africa."

"Yes," I say.

There is a long silence, the ticking is consuming. "I should go," I say.

"I'm Maud," she says, and holds out her hand.

"Elena," I say. Her hand is warm and powdery.

"Stay until eleven, that's only seven minutes away."

So for seven minutes we talk, about her grandfather, who owned the store, her children, one of whom is in heaven, about the crazy Bayous, where she was born, and about a local lake I should go swimming in.

And then the clocks begin to chime, beginning with a low grandfather clock and joined by other grandfather clocks and old-fashioned desk clocks and so many others all chanting out tones in all different cadences, church bells, ominous tick-tocking deep and low, bright cuckoo clocks rasping and screaming all at once, all exactly on the hour, so that I am shattered and held fast and bound at their existence, at the fact that one or two minutes have passed, and then they resume their clicking, in and out of phase, surrounding us, like rain.

Maud's face is arched back, her eyes closed.

Then she looks at me, her eyes like a blue wave.

"Wasn't that beautiful?" she asks.

And it was. It was as though time had stopped, was forever standing still, waving in the breeze, rooted forever.

Maud pushes up her sweater sleeves and there is a tattoo in a ring around her wrist.

I suddenly want to be free of everything.

"I have something from Africa," I blurt out. I didn't even really mean to say that.

"Oh?"

"Yes," I say. "Follow me."

And so I take her to my car and point to the long box.

"A tusk," I say.

"Oh."

"For the sunglasses," I say.

The light is dappled in the trees above us and a faint breeze blows through her dry hair. She is looking at me, studying me, and swallowing. She keeps swallowing. I try to imagine what she looked like when she was younger and I can't. She is old and wrinkled and it seems crazy that that will happen to me, and after a few seconds I have to look away and just remember the sound of the clocks, the way that each sound hit a different part of my body like I was a drum. We are under the shifting dappling light beneath a tree and when I look back her eyes are bright, like she has been crying, but she hasn't, and then she finally answers me, with just a nod.

"But you can't sell it," I say. "It's only for display. If you sell it, they will kill another elephant. Do you understand that?" I ask her.

She is looking at the casket.

"You burn it, before you die. You burn it. Can you do that?" I ask her.

"I don't know."

"Promise me."

She looks at the ground. "I promise," she says.

I wait by the car, and she goes to the back of her store to get her son and his wife. They all come out, nondescript and worn; gray corduroy pants and a ripped white t-shirt on him and red warm-ups and tank top on her, and both of them with brown eyes, her eyes looking browner under her bleached-out hair, and I just stand there with the sound of the clocks cascading and falling, still clear, still right here. The guy looks at the scratched and wasted coffin and back at his mother like she's crazy and then he starts pushing from the passenger floor and the girl in red is supposed to hold the top.

"I'll do it if it's too heavy," I tell her.

The coffin is actually very shiny compared to how it was, and it plays with the light we are under, turning amber and dark, flashing between the scratches and worn patches.

The girl mumbles something and hunches over the end of the coffin, like she's worried she's going to drop it. She doesn't look strong.

They manage to haul it away from the car and over to the sidewalk, the wife making small sounds in her throat. I could walk a mile holding one end of it, and I'm annoyed she thinks it so difficult. Maud is standing under the tree watching them, not saying a word, holding the aviator glasses.

I like Maud, but I'm not sure about the other two. I should change my mind. This is just another mistake. Watching the girl in red squeaking down the sidewalk with my mother's coffin is just like standing around watching the burning man die.

I slam down my trunk. I slam it hard.

I look at Maud. Her eyes look like deep holes. I can't breathe very well.

Maud has the sunglasses in front of her stomach. I hold out my hand for them.

She pushes them, very slowly, into the air in front of her. I take them. They have leather side covers and mirror fronts and they are heavy, for sunglasses, and I put them on, and like a flood of African gold light, they make the streets glowing and warm.

I can't breathe, so I get in the car. The space around me feels light and empty and absent, like I'm not even here. I desperately miss the coffin, like a phantom limb, and I can't turn on the engine to the car, I can't move.

It occurs to me that all of my momentum was dependent on the tusk, because I can't even reach for the door handle. I can't move at all, and the inner, invisible trembling has reentered my body, adrenalin and fear resettling. The tusk was my calm, the tusk was my easiness, not the money, and everything tells me to go back, go back and get the tusk.

They have all disappeared into the shop door. They are probably trying to open the coffin right now. It feels like an irrevocable violation; it feels like a new trap. And then out of nowhere I feel it, a wild thrashing in my stomach, in my chest, and the whole car seems to be a whirlwind of activity, blood splattering, my sight turning cloudy; I want to fling myself through the windshield, or tear out my throat, and just like the hyena ripping out his intestine for the pain, I think, I've finally done it, I've finally ripped out all of what is inside of me and now I've expired, alone, longing for something unknown, on a strange street in my ratty car.

I manage to push open the car door against the implacable heat, and I walk through a torrent of humidity, fighting me all the way to her door.

The cow bells ring against the glass. All three of them are standing over the coffin. It is already open, and the son kicks it shut as I walk toward them.

A thin whisp of anger boils up in me. I'm ready for battle. They should not have opened it.

"I changed my mind," I say. "I need the coffin back."

"You can't do that," he says.

"Yes I can," I say, staring into his placid face.

"She can," Maud says.

"No, she can't. It was an even trade."

I don't stop looking at him. I place the sunglasses on the glass countertop.

"Here are your brother's glasses," I say. "Please help me carry my mother's coffin back to my car."

His mouth moves to say something, but Maud puts her hand on his shoulder.

"Do it," she whispers in his ear.

"But—"

"Do it," she whispers again.

As soon as I touch the coffin I feel a surge of strength.

"Don't drop it," I say, and smile at him.

He is sour-faced all the way down the sidewalk.

"I got it," I say at the end. He is sweating; his shirt is wet.

I wedge the coffin in myself, as quickly as I can, and tie the trunk.

Then I focus on finding Interstate 40, and once I find it I don't stop for anything except gas, for another seventeen hours.

Once I enter New Mexico I lean back a little, and in the soft black sky Venus is rising. For a second, I see Elena in her white Dior dress. The air is thin and dry and windy. I pass truckers pulled over on the side of the road, and I'm pleased that I outlasted them. They must have pulled over at three or four in the morning. I reach the city at dawn and park under my window.

I live on the second floor of a pathetic apartment building, over-looking the parking lot and a graveyard. The blackbirds are awake, a few are in the parking lot, eating crumbs. I'm exhausted. At first the asphalt rolls under my feet in that annoying way, and then I know how to move again, and I take my keys and go upstairs. The build-ing is quiet. I unlock my door. The room is almost unfamiliar. My plants are dead, and I wonder how I could have been in such a state as to leave without securing someone to water them. I should have told the landlord to water them when I called in and sent the checks.

There are color xeroxes of petroglyphs all over the floor. The air is dusty and close. I walk over the images and open the window and look down at my car. I'll bring the coffin up myself. I prop open my door with a book and shove a stick in the hinge of the door to the building.

I've always enjoyed moving furniture around. When I was a kid, I used to move my bed every week or so. I pretend this will be easy. The coffin is really just a long rectangle, one hundred and forty pounds. I push it out and prop it against the car. If I push it across the parking lot it will get scratched, so I run upstairs, grab a blanket, lay the blanket down on the asphalt, and lower the coffin down on top of that. The blanket won't move. But the coffin will slide over that, so I slide it to the other side of the blan-ket and start again. The sides of the coffin are getting scraped, but I manage to get it through the front door and to the base of the steps.

The carpeting in the hallways and on the stairs is a rough, dis-gusting brown. I spread the blanket over the steps and lift and push. The coffin catches at the beginning of each step so I have to push down to decrease the drag. It is slow-going, up each stair, pause, push. The insides of my arms are scraped and stinging. I begin to hate the thing as much as I want it.

For several moments I just sit, with the box at my back, threatening to slide through my back and crash to the floor below. I turn around and use all of my leg strength to push it up to the first landing. The stairs are in two sections, and I sit on the coffin for several minutes, between the flights of stairs. People in the apartment building are waking up—I hear muffled voices and showers running—and I'd rather no one saw me with the box.

My legs are shaking when I stand up again. Getting it to lie along the stairs is the hard part. I lift and push and lift and push for a while. Then in one long continuous and muffled scream I push the coffin up the rest of the steps.

You son of a bitch, I say to it, *you son of a bitch.*

My back aches and my arms are bleeding.

Then I push it along the hallway and into my room just enough so I can slam the door and lock it.

I collapse on my bed.

I wake up in the middle of the night, dying of thirst. The water in the tap is sour. I've always hated Albuquerque water. I take the hottest shower possible for as long as the water holds out, which is a very long time. Then I change my sheets and dust off the windowsill and fall back asleep.

When I wake up again, it is still dark out but the sun is about to rise. The trees and the corners of the buildings are edged with light.

The petroglyphs on my floor are wrinkled and disordered. I pick them all up and stack them in piles. In my research I discovered that the most common petroglyphs, found throughout the world, are drawings of a bird on a stick, and men with spears. You find these drawings on every continent. But covering my floor are mostly squiggly lines and spirals. Spirals are most common in the American Southwest. I've always thought spirals were meant to take someone in and out of time. Maybe that's why I've never liked them. I stack the xeroxes on a closet shelf.

With the floor clear I push the coffin over to the side of the room. It is a studio apartment, so there isn't a lot of extra space. I have a bed and a table, and now, a coffin. I'm surprisingly happy with it. I decide to push it over to the window to make a window seat.

I have a craving for one of those small cold bottles of grape juice, and I decide to walk over to 7–Eleven to get one. It's going to be hot today, I can tell already.

I take my time getting ready to leave, trying on all my old clothes. I don't like any of them. I choose my shorts and bikini top with a tank top over that.

I start walking, already feeling the heat dissipate the cool air. Around here, every street has a back alley, and I know them all. There's a whole mini-city, a shadow grid of roads, some dirt and some paved, and I zigzag through them in the direction of my grape juice.

I pass the yard across from the white apartment complex and there are an inordinate number of dirty rawhide dog bones. And on the telephone wire above me, a whole line of blackbirds, all facing the same direction, calling softly. I stare at them for a while. There must be fifty birds, all in a line, all facing east. Then I switch my course at the new Kinko's and step over the low chain at the edge of the parking lot.

I take a different alley, one that runs all the way through, so that I end up on the other side of Zuni, behind the used bookstore with its racks of old, sun-faded books and magazines, and I loop around to the 7–Eleven.

In the fluorescent light of the refrigerator is my grape juice. I take a cold glass bottle and pay and leave. I hold off drinking it.

I double back and enter the short alley that forces me into the Burger King parking lot. Police sirens scream in the distance as I walk across, and I measure the time between sirens, suddenly terrified that in the next second I will see the burning man, and I wonder how this has come to be. But I continue in motion, through what feels like a swirling portal of time, my feet crunching the gravel in the flowerbeds by the order intercom. I can hear the cars and sirens on Central Avenue. I walk over and stare at what is left of the burn marks from the beginning of summer, and I think about the way I did nothing, the way I thought my actions were inconsequential.

I don't feel that way now. With the heat of the day coming on, I walk across the asphalt and into a dusty alley. In each step, I feel a vast mystery, and with each step, a dynamic precision.

The siren is closer now, like I'm in a center point, where all the alleys and streets converge. I open the grape juice and drink in a silvery sweetness and rush of cold. Blackbirds are flying overhead. I look back down the alley, and there, zooming between the streets, Michael's turquoise truck, a sun-burnished blue, a steady stream, skimming in and out of view. I inhale and circle around, anticipating where he might end up, tracking the blue.

SOURCES

Beard, Peter H. 1988. *The End of the Game.* San Francisco: Chronicle Books.

Chadwick, Douglas H. 1992. *The Fate of the Elephant.* San Francisco: Sierra Club Books.

Douglas-Hamilton, Iain and Oria. 1975. *Among the Elephants.* London: Collins & Harvill Press.

Harrison, Gordon. 1978. *Mosquitoes, Malaria & Man.* New York: E. P. Dutton.

Jenner, Edward. 1996. *Vaccination Against Smallpox.* New York: Prometheus Books. (Originally published between 1798-1800; in New York 1910, P.F. Collier & Son.)

Matthiessen, Peter. 1991. *African Silences.* New York: Vintage Books, Random House.

Moss, Cynthia. 1992. *Echo of the Elephants.* New York: William Morrow and Company, Inc.

Orenstein, Ronald. Editor. 1991. *Elephants, The Deciding Decade.* San Francisco: Sierra Club Books.

Preston, Richard. *The New Yorker.* July 12, 1999. *The Demon in the Freezer. The New Yorker* by Conde Nast Publications Inc., NY. Vol. LXXV, No. 18, July 12, 1999.

ACKNOWLEDGMENTS

Special thanks in more or less chronological order to: my parents, who gave me everything they had; Miranda for being the only one who really understands my sense of humor; Bozanic for his leather jacket and cigarettes and passion for Eliot and Pound and an acute reading of *Desire* years ago; Mrs. Sharp for teaching me discipline and categorical thinking; Deirdre for playing me "Get Off of My Cloud" and knowing how to talk in code; Serena for her ceaseless fire and hunger and a love of yellow raisins; Mark for the chains and the forest; Aaron for wanting to know something about everything; Kaye for her mystery; Kurth for teaching me J.B.; Vint for slamming into a ditch on a late night highway; Noah, who must know what they're talking about because he gave me V. Morrison, Al Green, Aretha, & religious Dylan, not to mention Cassavettes, Godard, & Antonioni; Destiny for always being there, for always reading everything, for always being honest, and for living all the way; Anderson, for his lightning connections; S. Feschbach for his easy and interminable knowledge; Ron & Lisa for late night conversations and unquenchable enthusiasm; Mike DeVito for his art and music; David for being our dog; Robert for getting us work and taking us to the magic river in NYC; Tuten for being a dinosaur with me; Mirsky for his mystic quest; L. Abrams for her diplomacy; Gail for her quickness of mind; Kevin for his generosity; Laird for standing on the sidewalk one night and telling me to send my work to Chris; Paula & Angie and their babies for keeping me company when Kelt was only a few months; Ernesto for his forthright honesty and support; Linda Allen for her early encouragement; Louise Quayle for taking a chance and for that one line at the graveyard; Lee Boudreaux for reading an unsolicited manuscript and giving me excellent criticism; Stacey D'Erasmo, who made me see narrative structure in three dimensions; Sandra Benitez for her kindness; Jennifer Katz, who knows how to party and work and talk all night long and whose support in our lives has been invaluable; Maya, our muse; Jill, for including me; Susann Cokal for her luscious book and our e-mail correspondence; Abby Frucht and Fanny Howe for their work and their blurbs; Sam, for his violating prose & poetry & his generous parents; Jamie Callan, for her daring; Summer & Margi & Laurie & Cathy & Amy, all friends who helped me survive home schooling & writing at the same time; Louis, forever and for always; Kelt for his quiet knowing; Van for his humor and stories; and all those people I haven't mentioned, whose art and thoughts I've encountered and loved. And thanks especially to Chris and Allan of Coffee House, who said yes, and their colleagues, Molly and Linda, for seeing it through. And thanks to my readers for reading.

FUNDER ACKNOWLEDGMENTS

Coffee House Press is an independent nonprofit literary publisher. Our books are made possible through the generous support of grants and gifts from many foundations, corporate giving programs, individuals, and through state and federal support. Coffee House Press has received support from the Minnesota State Arts Board, through appropriations by the Minnesota State Legislature and by the National Endowment for the Arts, a federal agency; and from the Elmer and Eleanor Andersen Foundation; the Buuck Family Foundation; the Bush Foundation; the Grotto Foundation; the Lerner Family Foundation; the McKnight Foundation; the Outagamie Foundation; the John and Beverly Rollwagen Foundation; the law firm of Schwegman, Lundberg, Woessner & Kluth, P.A.; Target, Marshall Field's, and Mervyn's with support from the Target Foundation; James R. Thorpe Foundation; West Group; the Woessner Freeman Foundation; and many individual donors.

Good books are brewing at coffeehousepress.org